Tattered & Torn

a quilting cozy

Carol Dean Jones

Publisher: Amy Marson

Creative Director: Gailen Runge

Acquisitions Editor: Roxane Cerda

Managing Editor: Liz Aneloski

Project Writer: Teresa Stroin

Technical Editor / Illustrator:
Linda Johnson

Cover/Book Designer: April Mostek

Production Coordinator:
Zinnia Heinzmann

Production Editor: Jennifer Warren

Photo Assistant: Mai Yong Vang

Cover photography by Lucy Glover and
Mai Yong Vang of C&T Publishing, Inc.

Cover quilt: *Tattered & Torn*, 1958,
by Vivien Bartling

Published by C&T Publishing, Inc.,
P.O. Box 1456, Lafayette, CA 94549

Library of Congress Cataloging-in-Publication Data

Names: Jones, Carol Dean, author.

Title: Tattered & torn : a quilting cozy / Carol Dean Jones.

Other titles: Tattered and torn

Description: Lafayette, California : C&T Publishing, [2019] | Series: A quilting cozy series ; book 9

Identifiers: LCCN 2018003522 | ISBN 9781617457364 (softcover)

Subjects: LCSH: Quilting--Fiction. | Retirees--Fiction. | Retirement communities--Fiction. | GSAFD: Mystery fiction.

Classification: LCC PS3610.O6224 T38 2018 | DDC 813/.6--dc23

LC record available at https://lccn.loc.gov/2018003522

POD Edition

A Quilting Cozy Series

by Carol Dean Jones

Tie Died (book 1)

Running Stitches (book 2)

Sea Bound (book 3)

Patchwork Connections (book 4)

Stitched Together (book 5)

Moon Over the Mountain (book 6)

The Rescue Quilt (book 7)

Missing Memories (book 8)

Tattered & Torn (book 9)

Left Holding the Bag (book 10)

Beneath Missouri Stars (book 11)

Frayed Edges (book 12)

Acknowledgments

I want to express my sincere appreciation to four very special friends: Joyce Frazier, Janice Packard, Sharon Rose, and Phyllis Inscoe, all of whom have spent hours reading these chapters, bringing plot inconsistencies and errors to my attention, and providing me with endless encouragement. Thank you, dear friends, for all your hard work and for bringing fun and friendship to what could otherwise have been a tedious endeavor.

I also wish to thank Bonnie Hunter for supplying the photograph of the vintage quilt that provided guiding inspiration for the *Tattered & Torn* story line. I recommend that you stop in for a visit at Bonnie's blog (quiltville.blogspot.com), which offers quilting tips and techniques, patterns and tutorials, and lots of quilting fun!

I also want to thank my readers. Many of you have stayed with me for the long haul, following Sarah and her cohorts from the beginning. I love hearing from you and hope you will contact me or visit me on my website.

Chapter 1

"Do you know anything about this old quilt?" Sarah asked as she gently ran her fingers over the delicate pattern, hesitant to even pick it up for fear it might crumble. "It looks very old."

"My guess would be that it's fifty or sixty years old," the shopkeeper responded, "but I don't know anything about it. It just came in a couple of weeks ago, and I haven't had a chance to examine it closely."

Sarah didn't make a habit of trolling thrift shops like her many friends in the retirement community where she lived, but this quilt had caught her eye as she was strolling past the shop on her way to meet her friend Sophie at the nearby café.

The shopkeeper carefully picked the quilt up and spread it out across an equally old upholstered wing chair. "The fabrics appear to be old, but I'm really not very knowledgeable about quilts. If you're interested in it, you might want to talk to someone in the quilt shop up the street." She slipped her glasses on and looked at it more closely. "Look at these tiny stitches," she said. "I haven't had it appraised," she added thoughtfully, "but I probably should before selling it."

Sarah examined the quilt carefully, noting places where the fabrics had partially disintegrated and other places where patterns were faded beyond recognition. She thought about the woman who had tediously pieced the quilt using scraps from her family's worn-out clothing. *It's amazing it has lasted this long*, she thought as she carefully lifted an edge to examine the back.

"I'd like to buy it," she found herself saying. The two women discussed it and ultimately agreed on a price, despite the shopkeeper's hesitance to sell it. Sarah had already begun wondering whether she could make the necessary repairs.

As she was leaving the shop with her carefully wrapped bundle securely tucked under her arm, Sarah turned to the shopkeeper and asked, "How did you happen to come by this quilt?"

"A woman brought it to me just a few weeks ago. She said her husband found it in the attic of an old building they were demolishing—part of the downtown revitalization program. They're tearing down public housing and replacing it with high-priced condominiums."

"I've read about that, and I've wondered where the people who were living there were going …" Sarah replied thoughtfully.

"To shelters and the streets would be my guess," the woman responded.

"The whole thing doesn't leave me feeling particularly *revitalized*," Sarah replied with a sigh as she left the shop and headed for the café.

On the way, Sarah passed the quilt shop and decided to stop in for a minute and show the quilt to her friend Ruth, the owner of Running Stitches.

"I only have a minute," Sarah began as she opened the bag and laid the quilt on the counter still folded. "I'm meeting Sophie, but I wanted you to see this. The owner of the shop said it was probably fifty or sixty years old."

"Sarah, you have a real treasure here, and I'm surprised Florence didn't realize what she had. From these fabrics, I'd say this quilt dates back to the mid-1800s, probably before the Civil War."

"Really?" Sarah gasped. "She said it's a hexagon quilt. Did they make them that long ago?"

"Hexagon quilt patterns became popular back in the 1700s, and there are many different layouts and names—the most common being this pattern, Grandmother's Flower Garden. And these fabrics were very common during the Civil War period. This is an exciting find, Sarah."

"Would you help me figure out how to repair it?"

Ruth hesitated. "I'd be happy to talk with you about it, but you might not want to disturb its authenticity."

Sarah was eager to continue the conversation, but at that moment several customers were entering the shop. Sarah knew Sophie was probably becoming impatient, so she slipped the quilt back into the bag and told Ruth she'd be back.

"Come by early in the morning," Ruth said as her friend was leaving, and Sarah nodded her agreement.

* * * * *

"That thing is in shreds!" her boisterous buddy bellowed when Sarah revealed the contents of her package. "Why would you pay good money for that rag? I could have given you something I use in Emma's dog bed if I had known you wanted something like this."

"Sophie, this *rag* as you call it is a piece of our history. It may well be a priceless antique."

"*Priceless* is right. There's no price a sane person would pay for it."

Sophie was new to the world of quilting, and Sarah knew to be patient with her, but she was finding it challenging. She repackaged her treasure and over lunch began sharing some of the stories she had heard about quilts created during the Civil War period.

Sarah told her friend about how fancy quilts were made and sold to raise money for the war effort and how simpler quilts were made as cot quilts for sons and husbands as they headed out to join the fighting. When she got to the part about how often the bodies of their loved ones were wrapped and buried in these simple quilts, Sophie became quiet. "Sorry," she muttered contritely. "I didn't know."

"Very few quilts made in that period have survived; if this is truly one of them, it's a real treasure. I just wish I knew more about its history."

Sophie was quiet as they drove home, and Sarah knew to give her friend the space she needed. As Sophie was getting out of the car, she turned to Sarah and said, "If you want to find out where this quilt came from, I'd like to help you."

"Great," Sarah responded enthusiastically. "The Sarah-Sophie investigation team is on the job."

Sophie threw her head back and cackled, instantly returning to her usual outrageous self. "We're going to be detecting again. Shall I bring my gun?"

"Sophie, you know you don't have a gun, and we wouldn't need it for this job even if you did."

Chapter 2

The following morning, Sarah pulled up to Running Stitches twenty minutes before Ruth arrived to unlock the door. Sarah tried the knob even though the closed sign was posted, hoping that Ruth might already be inside. It was indeed locked. She was eager to see Ruth and get her professional advice regarding making repairs to her quilt.

Sarah impatiently paced for a few minutes then decided to cross the street and attempt to relax with a cup of coffee. Sitting at a window booth so she could watch for Ruth, she opened the bag and pulled the tissue aside to look at the quilt again. It was a bright sunny day, and she told herself hopefully, *It doesn't look so bad in this light.*

"You'd better get that out of the sunshine," the voice behind her announced cheerfully. Startled, Sarah turned to see that Ruth was standing by her table.

"I can hardly wait for you to see the entire quilt," Sarah responded excitedly, tucking the tissue around the quilt.

"Let's head on over to the shop so we can spread it out before the customers start arriving."

As they walked across the street, Sarah asked if Ruth knew the owner of the thrift shop well.

"Florence? I've known her for years. She opened her shop at the same time I opened Running Stitches. We met at the city zoning office when both of us were arguing the same issue. We were able to help each other through the process, and we both got what we wanted. We celebrated with lunch at Cucina's, and we've made it a tradition to celebrate our shops' anniversaries there every year. So tell me about the quilt."

"It has some serious problems, but I'm hoping you can guide me through the repairs. You'll see when we spread it out. I'm excited about it, but mostly I want to know more about it. I'm hoping you can tell me something about its past."

"What kind of damage does it have?" Ruth asked.

"Well, there are a few serious holes. Some of the fabrics—particularly the reds—have faded, and other fabrics are disintegrating. I can replace those, but I want to find some vintage fabrics for the replacements, and I want to use the right kind of thread. There are also a few tears that go all the way through to the back. And, of course, there are places where the stitches have dissolved." Sarah sighed as she began to realize the enormity of the project. "The binding will need to be replaced, too, but again I'll want to find the right vintage fabric."

"You said you want to repair the quilt, but I'm beginning to wonder if you aren't, in fact, talking about restoring it."

"I don't know the difference, Ruth. That's what I'm hoping you'll help me with."

They had just entered the shop, and Ruth began her opening rituals. "Why don't you go spread it out in the classroom? We can examine it there without being interrupted. Anna will be in shortly, and she can take over in the shop." Anna, Ruth's younger sister, had moved to Middletown hoping to build family connections now that she and her husband had children.

Just as Ruth got the lights on and the cash register set up, a group of women pulled up in a van and burst through the door. "We need backs and battings for our charity quilts," one of the women announced as they entered. "And I need blades for my rotary cutter," one of the other women added. Ruth tucked her purse under the counter and began helping the women. She learned the group of friends had gotten together to make quilts for the women's shelter in town. "We started out just making them for the beds in the shelter, but we discovered that the women loved them. We three have more fabric than we can ever use, so we started making extras, and now the women are able to take them when they move into their new homes."

"We can hardly keep up with the demand," one of the women added.

"Do you need some help?" Ruth asked. "Our Tuesday Night Quilters are always willing to take on charity projects."

"That's a very generous offer, Ruth," the older woman and apparent leader responded. "If we get in a bind, we'll take you up on that."

While they talked, Sarah headed for the classroom, where she placed the quilt in the supply cabinet instead of spreading it out until Ruth was available. The sun was streaming in across the worktable, and she knew Ruth would tell her not to put it there. She then hurried to the kitchen to make coffee. Ruth had handed her a bag of fresh bakery items, which Sarah arranged on a platter once she got the coffee started. The regular customers of Stitches knew to come into the kitchen and help themselves to refreshments.

A few minutes later, Sarah heard the jingle of the bell on the front door, and Anna came breezing in, carrying her new baby. "She's asleep," Anna announced. "I'll put her in the crib in the back, and she'll be fine for a couple of hours. Geoff is going to pick her up at noon after his class." Anna was an expert at balancing home, work, and children. Her older girl had already been delivered to day care, where she would stay until her father picked her up.

Ruth and Anna took care of several other customers while Sarah went back into the classroom and began spreading out the quilt.

Finally, Sarah and Ruth were alone in the classroom. The door was closed, the blinds tilted to avoid direct sunshine, and the quilt was spread out on the table. "It measures 44″ by 89″," Ruth was saying. "That's about the size that the Sanitary Commission recommended for cot quilts during the Civil War. That may have been the quilter's intention."

Sarah felt a shiver of excitement travel down her spine.

"On the other hand, most of the cot quilts were made in a hurry using blocks that went together quickly, and they were often tied rather than quilted. This flower garden design is very time-consuming to make, and it's been hand quilted instead of tied. That doesn't rule it out as a cot quilt, but it makes it seem less likely."

Ruth continued to examine the quilt closely, and she suddenly exclaimed, "Here's our answer. Look at the binding on this side."

"It's different than on the other three sides," Sarah responded. "I noticed that earlier, but I figured our quilter ran out of fabric."

"I don't think that's it," Ruth said slowly, beginning to form her idea. "I believe that this quilt was originally a bed quilt that was cut down the middle to make a cot quilt quickly—actually, *two* cot quilts."

"They did that?" Sarah was appalled.

"They sure did. Those were desperate times."

Sarah imagined gunfire in the background as her mind drifted off to a gray weathered shack and two women standing on the porch. Their arms were intertwined and their cheeks tearstained as they watched their boys trudging down the dusty road with their meager possessions strapped to their backs.

"Sarah? Are you with me?"

"Oh, sorry. I was just thinking about what you said."

"You look like there's something you want to say," Ruth said with a concerned look. She gently laid her hand on Sarah's arm and added, "Is something bothering you?"

Sarah took a deep breath and began. "I'm not sure how to explain this, Ruth. I feel," she hesitated, searching for the right words. "I feel very drawn to this quilt or perhaps to the woman who made it. I feel as if this quilt needs something from me, and I know that makes no sense at all."

"This quilt has really had an impact on you, hasn't it?"

"It has, and I don't understand it."

"Some people think that an inanimate object can hold energy from its past. I once met a woman who claimed she could sense messages from beyond the grave by simply touching the belonging of loved ones who had passed on, but I figured it was some sort of flimflam."

"It probably was," Sarah responded with a smile.

"My advice to you is that you don't try to dissect your feelings. Just enjoy this very special quilt that has somehow made its way to you."

It made its way to me? Sarah thought. *Interesting way to put it ...*

"So, back to the quilt," Ruth said as she carefully lifted a corner and peered at the back. "I assume there's no label, right?"

"Right, but there are the remnants of some embroidery thread. Let me show you." They carefully turned the quilt over, and Sarah searched for the wrinkled corner where she had seen the threads. "See? Right here. That looks like an *M* or maybe an *N*, and then there's some space. On a little farther is an *O* for sure, but I can't make out these three letters that are together."

Ruth reached for her magnifying glass and examined the area very carefully. "I can make out an *I* and an *E* and possibly an *S*. Grab that paper and write this down: *M* or *N*, space, space, *O*, space, *IES*. Does that look like anything?" she asked Sarah, who was now studying the area with the magnifying glass.

"Couldn't this be the beginning of another *M* right here before the *O*?" she asked, squinting into the glass. She pulled her glasses off and said, "There. That's better. That could definitely be another *M*."

"Memories!" Ruth cried abruptly, causing Sarah to almost drop the magnifying glass.

"Memories? Are you sure?" Sarah studied the area more closely. "I think you're right, and even if you aren't, this will be my *Memories* quilt from this day on. Let's look for a date."

There was no sign of a date and no evidence one had ever been added. "Now *this* is exactly why I keep telling people that their quilts are not finished until they've added the label," Ruth said, frowning. "Just think, if *Memories* had a label, we'd possibly know when it was made, where, and by whom." Sarah thought about all the quilts she had made; only one had a label. She made a personal vow to go back and add labels to all of them.

"Tell me what you have in mind for this quilt," Ruth said. "Are you hoping to restore it to as close to authentic condition as you can, or do you simply want to repair the damage? Are you going to use it? Display it? What will you be doing with this quilt?"

"I'll certainly display it. It's too delicate to use. But it doesn't have to be in original condition. I probably could never find fabrics that old."

"You could search through antique shops and even on the internet for old fabric, or you might find another old quilt in worse condition that could be cut up. And I've seen vintage squares from unfinished quilts that were pinned together and sold in antique shops. You could check with Florence about that. But I agree that you'd have a time finding fabrics that are at least a hundred and fifty years old. You could consider using Civil War–reproduction fabrics," Ruth added, "but you'd be making repairs, not restoring it."

"I guess I could," Sarah replied thoughtfully. "It all depends on how authentic I want it to be. This is going to require a great deal of thought."

The two women spent another hour going over the quilt and talking about how to make the various repairs if that's what Sarah decided to do. As she was leaving the shop, Sarah purchased a spool of silk thread just in case she decided to make a few small repairs.

* * * * *

"Did you know that Timothy and Martha are away?"

"What do you mean *away*?" Sarah asked her husband, Charles, who was standing in the kitchen looking perplexed when Sarah walked in.

"I just called Andy about playing golf tomorrow, and he said he and Caitlyn are taking care of Penny and Blossom for a few days. Do you know where they were going?"

"I have no idea. I haven't spoken to Martha for a week or so, and Sophie hasn't mentioned anything about her son being away."

Sarah's daughter, Martha, was not always forthcoming about her private life, but Timothy and Sophie had a much different relationship. "I'll give Sophie a call and ask her. Is Andy having a problem with Penny?"

"No. He wasn't complaining. He just mentioned it in passing and was surprised that we didn't know about it." Timothy, Sophie's son, and Andy, a friend and fellow resident of the village, had become supportive friends when they both found themselves single parents of teenage girls. Both girls had lost their mothers under very different circumstances and had come to live with their fathers. Not only had the fathers become friends, but their daughters had, as well.

"He did mention having problems with Penny's dog."

"Blossom? What kind of problems?"

"It seems Penny lets her get away with murder. Andy thinks the dog needs to be sent off to boot camp for some training."

"That's not the way it works," Sarah replied with a chuckle. "Timothy, Penny, and Blossom—all three—will need to be trained."

"So are you worried about Martha?" Charles asked his wife. She didn't seem to be concerned that they were away.

"Not at all," she replied. "They probably just needed some alone time. They've had a rough time with their relationship this year."

While visiting from Alaska, Timothy had met Sarah's daughter, Martha, at Sarah and Charles' wedding a couple of years back. Sarah and Sophie immediately saw the sparks fly, and for several months, they excitedly speculated that their two families might well become joined. But just as Timothy was preparing to retire and return to Middletown permanently, he learned that he had a fourteen-year-old daughter. The child's mother was dying and asked him to take her.

He returned to Middletown with the problem of adjusting to his new lifestyle: retirement, a new home, a teenage daughter, a girlfriend, and a small papillon. Unfortunately, his relationship with Martha took a back seat, and Sarah and Sophie began to think there was little hope it would survive. For one thing, Martha wasn't even sure she wanted to become a mother.

"In fact," Sarah continued, "this might be a good sign. Now that Tim's life is more settled and Martha has had time to get to know Penny, perhaps they can get their own relationship back on track. It could be difficult, though," she added thoughtfully. "There are sometimes bad feelings when a new relationship gets sidetracked."

"Let's not look for trouble," her sensible husband responded. "They'll be back in a few days, and I'm sure Martha will let us know what's going on."

"Maybe," Sarah replied. "She's always so secretive."

"She's a very private person, sweetheart. That's just who she is."

Sarah sighed and headed for her sewing room, thinking that she just might make a few small repairs to the quilt. She cleared off her worktable and spread it out so that she could examine it block by block. But she quickly changed her mind about making any repairs, not wanting to disturb the quilt in any way until she knew more about it.

She stood back and studied the quilt again. Something had been niggling at her since she first saw the quilt. *Maybe this quilt should go off to a museum, where curators can restore or conserve it*, she thought. "This could be an important piece of history," she said aloud.

"What did you say, hon?" Charles had been passing by the sewing room and caught her talking to herself. She decided to see what he thought.

"Come on in and take another look at this quilt. I want to ask you something."

As it turned out, Charles agreed that if the quilt turned out to be from the Civil War period, perhaps it should be shared with the world. "Will you be fixing it up first?"

"No. In that case, I wouldn't make any changes to it. The museum curator might restore it or perhaps just conserve it in its current condition; that would be their decision. But until I decide, I won't do any repairs. This will require some thinking. If it's really from the 1800s, it could be a significant piece deserving preservation. And if not, it's still a precious thing to own. In that case, I'd begin repairing it the best I can."

"It may actually be a piece of our history," Charles responded. "If it does end up in a museum, it would be good to have a plaque with it that explains who made it, when, and even why, but I guess no one knows any of that."

"You're right," Sarah replied. "No one knows any of that. But perhaps someone should find out." She looked at her husband, himself a retired detective; tilted her head to the side; and batted her eyelashes with exaggeration. "Don't you agree, dear?"

Charles laughed and shook his head in mock exasperation. "Here we go again. Detecting," he said. "But at least it doesn't involve murder this time."

Or so he hoped.

Chapter 3

"So have you started the repairs on your quilt?" Sophie asked. She and Sarah were sitting in her backyard sipping lemonade and watching the shenanigans of their two dogs, Emma and Barney. Emma, much younger than Barney, was attempting everything she knew about getting another dog to play, but Barney simply stretched out in the sun and pretended to be napping. She finally gave up and stretched out next to him.

"No. I've decided to hold off on repairs. I don't want to do anything to it until I decide whether I'm keeping it."

"What? You love that old thing," Sophie responded, looking perplexed. "Why wouldn't you keep it?"

Sarah told her about her concerns and the possibility of donating it to a quilt museum if it was, in fact, as old as they suspected. "But first I want to learn more about it."

"That's where I come in!" Sophie exploded with delight. "I've already had some ideas …"

"Hold on, Sophie. Before we get into that, I want to ask you something. Do you know where Martha and your son have gone?"

"Gone? Nowhere that I know of. Why do you ask?"

"Have you spoken to him lately?"

Sophie thought a minute and responded, "It was four or five days ago, but why do you ask?"

"Charles learned from Andy that he and Caitlyn are taking care of Penny and Blossom for a few days."

"What? Why didn't he leave her with me?" Sophie demanded. "I'm insulted! Where are they, anyway? I'm going to call Timothy right now." With a look somewhere between anger and worry—a look only a mother can produce—she pulled her phone out of her pocket and hit the button to call her son. "It's gone right to voice mail," she exclaimed. "He has it turned off. This is really annoying." The frown grew deeper. "I'm going to call Andy and find out what's going on." She started to dial, but Sarah laid her hand over the phone.

"Sophie, hold on. Don't forget your son and my daughter are adults, and they can go away for the weekend without accounting to us. Besides, I already spoke to Andy, and they didn't tell him where they were going, just that they'd be gone three days."

"What did they tell Penny?" Sophie asked.

"All Penny knows is that she was lucky enough to have a three-day sleepover with her best friend. Andy said that Penny was offered her choice and, like any teenager, she chose the place that would be the most fun."

"Humph." Sophie slid the phone back into her pocket and sighed. "I've been pushed entirely out of the loop."

"Now, Sophie, it's nothing personal, but I'm a little curious myself. You don't suppose …?" Sarah hesitated to finish the sentence, but it was too late, and Sophie caught on right away.

"Eloped? You think they eloped?" Sophie didn't wait for an answer but began huffing and muttering incoherently.

"I don't think so, but I suppose it's possible," Sarah responded. "Maybe they just didn't want a big fuss …"

"If that boy thinks he can do me out of this wedding, he's very much mistaken. Just wait 'til those two get back. I'll throw them the fanciest wedding party this town has ever seen. I'll rent the …"

"Sophie, stop. Calm down." Sophie was now pacing back and forth, completely forgetting her arthritis and practically tripping over Emma, who had become almost as agitated as Sophie.

"I'll fix those two. I'm calling the Beaumont right now and reserving their largest ballroom …"

Sarah interrupted her again, this time getting up and physically stopping her from pacing. "Sophie, we don't know that they've eloped. They probably are just taking a little time to themselves. That's what Charles thinks, and I agree. They haven't had any time just for the two of them for the past year. Now come sit down with me and let's talk rationally."

"Humph," Sophie sputtered, but she returned to her chair, and Emma relaxed in the grass at her feet.

"Why didn't they tell me?" Sophie muttered, not expecting an answer. "Just imagine how upset they'd be if they discovered we'd vanished from the face of the earth …"

"Sophie, they haven't exactly vanished. They made arrangements for Penny, so this was something planned. We'll just have to wait until they get back."

"Wait until they get back *married*, you mean."

"Sophie …"

"Just think about it, Sarah. Why else would they suddenly take off like this and not tell anyone? It's exactly what I did, and …"

"Exactly what *you* did?" Sarah asked, looking at her friend with astonishment. "You eloped?"

"Okay, I did, but that doesn't make it right. My parents acted as if they were angry, but now I know how they felt."

"Hurt?"

"Yeah," she responded, dropping her eyes and reaching down to scratch Emma's head. "Hurt."

"Since we don't know for sure that's what they did, could we just put this aside until they return? I was hoping we could talk about how we'll find out about the past life of my quilt."

Sophie sat quietly and appeared reluctant to let go of her mood, but finally Sarah could see the beginnings of her old twinkle. "I agree. I'd much rather talk about that, and I've had some thoughts about where to begin."

"Tell me."

"Okay," Sophie began with renewed enthusiasm. "You said some workman found the quilt in an attic. Let's find that man and get details. Once we know which attic, we might be able to find out who lived there last."

"Exactly," Sarah responded, delighted to see how quickly Sophie could set aside her concerns when there was the possibility of solving a mystery, big or small. "Let's go to the thrift shop and talk to Florence. I'm sure she keeps records and can tell us who brought the quilt in. We can start there."

"Today?" Sophie asked enthusiastically.

"Sure, if you want." Sarah hadn't planned to go today, but it would be the perfect way to distract her friend. "I'll go home and get some lunch, and we'll leave around 1:00. How's that?" Sarah suggested as she stood and headed for the kitchen door.

"I don't like it."

Sarah, startled by her friend's response, looked back at her and asked, "Why not?"

"Because I think we should eat out."

Sarah laughed and agreed. "Grab your purse and let's go right now. I'll call Charles and tell him he's on his own for lunch." Heading toward the car, both women were excitedly chattering about their plans. Elopement worries had been moved to a back shelf.

* * * * *

When Sarah returned, she found Charles sitting at his computer wearing his oldest sweatshirt and ragged jeans. She noticed that his shoes were covered with damp matted grass, and she spotted more under the computer table.

"You mowed I see."

"Oops. Sorry. I meant to clean up before I came in here, but I had this idea about your quilt and wanted to get on the computer and check it out."

"Really? What idea?"

"I was wondering if I could pull up pictures of quilts made during the 1800s and maybe find it."

Sarah chuckled. "Oh, that it could be that simple. I'd be surprised if anyone took the time to take a picture of this one and load it onto the internet, not to mention you'll find millions of quilt images."

"I've discovered that. How about you? Any luck?"

"It was just a first step. We went to the thrift shop and got the name and address of the woman who sold the quilt to Florence. I just need to find her phone number and arrange to go see her and her husband."

"Ah," Charles responded. "That gives me a more reasonable computer task." He hit a few keys and read the number to Sarah. "And, if you're interested, she's forty-eight years old and has three associates living at her address."

"There are no secrets anymore," Sarah muttered as she headed for her sewing room.

Charles followed her in and asked to see the quilt again.

"Not until you get cleaned up," she responded, looking at the trail of damp grass he had left behind.

A short time later, Charles appeared at the door to the sewing room freshly showered. "How's this?" he said, indicating his clean jeans and tee-shirt. "And I wiped up all the grass."

"I was just going to spread out the quilt," she responded with an appreciative smile. "Sophie wants a picture of it, and I was hoping you'd snap it and send it over to her smartphone."

"Sure will," he replied, pulling out his own phone. "I'm surprised she ever agreed to that purchase. It's so unlike your friend." Sophie's son had overruled his mother's firm conviction to never own a computer or a mobile phone. He bought her a smartphone and insisted that she work with him until she knew the basics. As it turned out, she loved trolling the internet and even joined a social network. Timothy ended up buying her an unlimited data plan and told her to have fun.

"What does she want the picture for?" Charles asked as he took shots from several angles.

"Sophie sets up what she calls her 'Detecting File.' We stopped in town so she could buy another pack of 3″ by 5″ cards."

"What does she do with the cards?"

"She writes down all the clues we find and then she shuffles them around, sorts them into piles, and pins them on her corkboard looking for the solution."

"Cute," he responded with a touch of sarcasm.

"Okay, Detective Parker. That sounded just a bit condescending. She enjoys it, and she learned it from some female-detective novels she reads."

"And does this ever work for your friend?"

"It keeps her busy," Sarah responded as she carefully folded the quilt, returned it to the cabinet, and pulled out her latest project.

Once the picture was on its way to Sophie, Charles sat down on the futon and watched Sarah as she organized the blocks she'd been working on. They were for a quilt she was making for his grandson in Colorado.

"Do you really think Jimmy will like this?" she asked.

Charles had gone with her to choose the fabric, and they had decided on a mixed sports theme. Using material that featured baseball, soccer, and football, Sarah had fussy cut scenes she thought Jimmy would like—particularly boys actively playing the sports and the equipment they used. She separated these blocks with a bright multicolored sashing and added colorful stars as cornerstones.

"I think any ten-year-old boy would be crazy about it," he responded, "and if I know my grandson, he will never outgrow it. He loves sports, unlike his dad—and his granddad, for that matter."

Looking serious, Sarah turned to him and said, "I talked to Sophie about Tim and Martha. She had no idea they were gone."

"Was she upset?"

"She was off the wall. She's sure they've eloped."

"Oh, I doubt that," Charles responded. "They wouldn't do that to Penny—at least I hope they wouldn't. She's had enough surprises this year."

"Yet it is a possibility, you know."

"I thought about it briefly, but I believe that they're both too sensible for that. They would want to get Penny used to the idea. In fact, I think Penny should be a part of any ceremony they would have, assuming marriage is even in their future. You know they haven't spent much time together this past year."

"Maybe, maybe not, Charles. We really don't know what they do."

"Point taken."

"We'll just have to wait and see," she added.

Charles stretched out on the futon and fell asleep while Sarah cut out Jimmy's quilt. An hour or so later, she saw him beginning to stir. "I'm going to put Jimmy's quilt aside and start some dinner. How about Italian tonight? I could make lasagna."

"I love the idea of Italian, but let's head over to Campanili's. We haven't been there for ages, and I'd hate to waste this shower," he chuckled.

"Two restaurant meals in one day—I love it," she responded. "I'll call for reservations, and I think I'll take a bubble bath and dress up for the occasion."

"Does that mean I have to wear a tie?"

She kissed his cheek and left the room.

"I guess that means yes."

Chapter 4

"Thank you for seeing us," Sarah was saying as Claudia Simpson led them into the small but comfortable living room.

"This is my husband, Thomas." Mr. Simpson glanced up, nodded, and returned to his newspaper.

Sarah had called the Simpsons and asked if she and Sophie could meet with them to ask some questions about the quilt. Claudia had said they knew very little but would be happy to have them come by in the evening when Tom got home. "He's the one that found it," she had said.

"Why are you so interested in that quilt?" Claudia asked once they were settled.

Sarah explained her interest in finding out its history and talked a little about Civil War quilts in particular. Thomas put his newspaper aside and began to look interested in the conversation. "Probably valuable," he ultimately interjected. "Maybe we should have hung onto it, Claudia."

Sarah wondered if she should offer to give it back to him, but Sophie saved the day by quickly speaking up. "Oh, that old rag isn't worth anything except perhaps for its sentimental value. I doubt that you got anything for it from the shop."

"We did, as a matter of fact," Claudia said. "The lady gave me twenty dollars."

"Fantastic, Mrs. Simpson. You're a sharp negotiator," Sophie responded, noticing that Thomas Simpson had settled back behind his newspaper.

Interrupting his reading, Sarah asked, "Mr. Simpson, could you tell me where you actually found it?"

"It was bundled up in brown paper and stuck up in the attic along with lots of other junk in this row house we pulled down. One of those old dilapidated places over on Second Street. I think they said it used to be public housing. Probably run by the Housing Commission."

"Is there any way you might be able to identify which house it was?"

"What good would that do you? The house is gone now."

"I might be able to find the person that lived there."

"Aren't you afraid they'll want it back?"

Thinking the man still had dollar signs bouncing around in his head, Sophie spoke up and said, "No problem. If they want it, they can have it. It's junk."

He sighed and picked up his newspaper again. "That whole block is mostly demolished," he said without lowering the paper. "But I'm working over there tomorrow. I'll see if the foreman has any kind of address or lot number."

"We'd appreciate that, Mr. Simpson. Thank you for helping us."

"No problem. The wife will give you a call."

As they were leaving, Sarah gave Mrs. Simpson her phone number and turned to admire her garden. They spent a few minutes discussing a local dogwood blight, and Sarah left, thanking Mrs. Simpson for her time.

On their way home, Sarah stopped by Running Stitches to catch Ruth up on the quilt saga and to buy a border for Jimmy's quilt. "I think I want something plain—perhaps a tone-on-tone in blue—but not too fussy. It's for a ten-year-old boy."

"I have just the thing," Ruth responded, "but would you consider green?" She led them to the shelf under the window where she had her *environments*, as she called them: fabric with trees, grass, rocks, sand, water, skies, and anything found in nature other than animals, which she had in another section. She pulled out the fabric with the grass design. "How about this?"

"I love it," Sarah responded excitedly. "Where there are boys and sports, there's usually grass."

"I like these rocks," Sophie said.

"Hmm. Now I'm wondering. Ruth, what do you think?"

"I can only point you to the collection. This has to be your choice," she responded. "I think a boy would like any of these, especially with the sports fabrics you purchased. Is that what this is for?"

"One and the same. Let's go with the rocks. I wouldn't want that myself, but it has a real *boy* look to it, and it won't detract from the sports blocks."

"Still no word from Timmy," Sophie murmured on the ride home.

"Nor Martha," Sarah responded.

"Tomorrow is day three."

"Yes."

"We'll know something soon."

"Yes."

They remained silent the rest of the way home, each lost in her own thoughts. As Sophie was getting out of the car, she turned and said, "Sorry about my meltdown yesterday. Even if they got married, it's their business. I don't want to be that kind of mother-in-law."

"Neither do I, Sophie. Neither do I."

"Call me when you hear from the Simpsons," Sophie called back as she closed the door and headed up the walk. Sarah could see Emma with her head under the curtain, panting with joy at the sight of her favorite person returning home.

* * * * *

"Mrs. Parker? This is Claudia Simpson."

"Good morning," Sarah responded cheerfully. "I'm glad to hear from you. Did your husband have any luck?"

"No one knows the names of the residents in that old area, but Thomas got the lot number for you, and he said for you to contact the Housing Commission. His foreman said for you to ask for Sonya Blackwell because she's the caseworker in charge of alternative placements for those folks, and she'll probably know who lived there."

"Excellent," Sarah said excitedly. "She might even know where the people are now, as well."

"Good luck," Mrs. Simpson said as they hung up.

Once Sarah called Sophie with the update, she dialed the number Mrs. Simpson had given her. Her call was answered by Ms. Blackwell herself.

Sarah explained what she was trying to do, and Ms. Blackwell was immediately interested. "My mother was a quilter," she said, "and so was my grandmother. I know how special these old quilts can become. Let me check my computer and see if I can give you a contact for the family that moved out of that unit."

Sarah was put on hold for so long that she was beginning to think they might have been disconnected. "Sorry about the delay," Ms. Blackwell finally said. "I was checking with the welfare office to see if they had anything on this woman. Unfortunately, neither of us have a forwarding address. Her name is Maud Templeton. She was living there with her mother, but I remember that the older woman died some time ago. I don't know what might have become of Maud once the city started demolition. She was pretty low functioning, and I suppose she could have ended up in one of the shelters. I doubt that she had the resources to leave town. I was her caseworker and met with her every six months while she was living there, but once the development was closed down, I didn't hear from her again."

Sarah listened silently to the very disappointing report. "That's discouraging," she responded once Ms. Blackwell was finished. "What happens to these people who have been displaced?"

"We're able to find housing for some. I offered to help Maud, but she never returned to my office once she was evicted. I just assumed she'd moved in with someone, but now that I look at her record, I'm reminded that she didn't have much in the way of family. Her daughter died some years ago, and two of her grandsons, Jerome and Darnell, were in prison when I last saw her. I think there was one more boy, but I don't even have his name. Sorry I can't be of more help."

"I appreciate all you've done. At least I have a name, and that's a place to start."

"Let me know if you find her and she wants help," Ms. Blackwell added. "We've developed several new resources for the displaced tenants."

"I sure will, and thank you, Ms. Blackwell."

Sarah picked up the phone and dialed Sophie to tell her what she had learned, but before she could say a word, Sophie blurted out, "They're home, and I'm on my way to see that son of mine." Sophie hung up before Sarah could say another word.

Chapter 5

Sarah and Charles were sitting in the living room sipping coffee and watching their favorite morning news channel when there was a knock at the door, followed immediately by the door swinging open and Sarah's daughter, Martha, bursting into the room.

"Mom, I'm so sorry," she cried. "Sophie told me how frantic and upset you were when you couldn't find me. I never intended to cause you such …"

Sarah laughed and got up to embrace her daughter. "Martha, calm down. I wasn't frantic at all. I was concerned and maybe a little annoyed, but I certainly wasn't frantic."

"But Sophie said …"

Charles chuckled at that point and said, "I know what happened. Sophie took it very hard, and you got her version of how your mother reacted, right? The only frantic person was Sophie."

"I'm relieved to hear that," Martha responded, looking somewhat calmer. "But still, I'm really sorry. We should have talked to both you and Sophie. It's just that, well, I guess we just wanted to keep it between the two of us. I guess we just weren't ready to talk about what we were planning."

Charles saw a flicker of concern cross his wife's face. *Could Sophie have possibly been right?* they were both thinking as they shared a pondering look.

"Let me put a fresh pot of coffee on," Sarah said as she stood, "and let's sit down in the kitchen and talk about this."

"Shall I let you girls talk privately?" Charles asked, not sure whether to follow them.

"I'm not sure ..." Sarah responded, not knowing just what Martha wanted.

"It's fine, Charles," Martha said, walking over and giving him a hug as he stood up. "This involves the whole family."

Once they were seated around the table, each with a cup of coffee and a slice of the coffee cake Sarah had baked earlier that morning, Martha sighed and said, "Well, to begin with, you both know that Tim and I were contemplating marriage last year."

"Sophie was sure you had eloped," Sarah said. She saw an odd look on her daughter's face, which caused Sarah to add, "Is that what you want to tell us?"

Martha laughed and responded, "No. Thank goodness, because it sounds like Sophie was planning to make us pay dearly if we had done that. But Tim and I did talk about it, and we both knew that wasn't the right thing to do for a number of reasons. Our primary concern was getting past some of the issues that have come up since Tim moved back here."

"So you decided to go away together and talk about it?" Sarah asked.

"No. We thought that going away together would just muddy the waters and make it even harder to know what we wanted."

"So where have you been?" Charles asked, unable to wait patiently until Martha got to the point.

"I told Tim I wanted the two of us to go talk with Pastor John." Pastor John was not the family's current pastor but rather the pastor of the church the children had grown up in when their father was living. "You know how I feel about him," she added.

"I think that was an excellent idea," Sarah responded with a barely visible sigh of relief. "Was he able to help?"

"He sure was, Mom. He told us about a couples retreat over on Peoria Lake, and we decided to go. We attended workshops on communication and group discussions on marriage. They also had some recreational activities. We enjoyed the nature trails and even took a horseback ride."

"That's over by the Illinois River, isn't it?" Charles asked.

"Yes. There's a retreat complex there with cabins, a lodge with a dining room, and large rooms for workshops. It was a beautiful setting, particularly at night."

"And did you two find it helpful?" Sarah asked, joining her husband now in wanting to get to the bottom line.

"More than helpful, Mom. We were able to talk about our feelings and our concerns privately and with other couples. And I think we both have a better understanding of what we've each been grappling with."

"I'm glad, Martha. Communication is always the key."

"I know that now. I told Tim things that he wasn't aware of, like my fear of parenting at this stage of my life. We agreed that we're in this together."

"And the future?" Sarah asked cautiously.

"We're going to be just fine, but I know that Tim wants to be with me when we make any announcements about our future. I won't say anything now except to tell you that we've come to grips with the problems we had." Winking at her mother, she then added, "And we're excited about our future."

Sarah and Martha stood up at the same time and walked into each other's arms, both beginning to tear up. Charles stood as well but appeared uncomfortable by the women's emotional outpourings until Martha turned and hugged him as well.

"Have you explained all this to Sophie?" Sarah asked as they were walking toward the front door.

"Tim is there now. I'm heading over there as well. Hopefully, it's going well. When she exploded into Tim's house yesterday, she wouldn't listen to a word we had to say. She was furious with both of us."

"She was worried, Martha, and hurt because Tim didn't tell her he would be away. You know she's been without a family for many years, and suddenly she has a son, a granddaughter, a potential daughter-in-law, and a dog. She's still trying to catch up with her own emotions."

"We'll never do that to her again. Or you, either. It was thoughtless." She kissed them both goodbye and hurried out to her car.

When Sarah knocked on Sophie's door a few hours later, she wasn't sure what she would find. She had hoped Sophie would call after Tim and Martha left, but when she didn't hear from her, Sarah decided to stop by and get the histrionics over with. Much to her surprise, however, Sophie opened the door with a cheerful greeting and invited her into the backyard, where she had been sitting with Emma and drinking lemonade. "I'll grab a box of cookies," Sophie said as they passed through the kitchen.

Once they were settled in their favorite chairs, chatting amicably about the weather, the dogs, and the proposed outdoor community swimming pool, Sarah decided to open the topic of the elephant in the backyard. "So you talked with Tim?"

"I did," she responded calmly. "I wish they had told us before they left and saved us all that worry, but it was good news. I'm very proud of them for taking this route, and I'm sure there'll be a wedding before too long. He said they weren't ready to make an announcement, but he had a twinkle in his eye that told me it's not far away."

The two friends sat quietly for a few minutes, sipping their lemonade. "So," Sophie began, totally changing the subject, "what did you learn from Sonya Blackwell?"

Sarah brought her up to date, and they discussed where they might go from there. "Let's check out the shelters and see if they know Maud," Sophie suggested. "How many shelters are there?"

"Well, I only know of the one run by the city. But I'm sure there are a number of different shelters run privately, probably by the local churches. We could ask at the city shelter. They might know how to find the others."

"Good idea," Sophie responded, "and why don't you ask Charles to see what he can find out about shelters on the internet?"

"Even better idea," Sarah replied. "Are you free Wednesday? I thought perhaps we could spend the day looking for Maud Templeton."

"Free as a breeze. Let's do it."

* * * * *

"I'm excited about our adventure tomorrow," Sophie was saying as the two women pulled up in front of Stitches later that day. The Tuesday Night Quilters began at 7:00 after Ruth closed the shop, but several familiar cars were already parked along the street.

As Sophie was getting out of the car, Ruth opened the door to the shop and called to Sarah. "Hurry in. I have found some fabulous information for you."

When Sarah entered the shop a few minutes later, Ruth led her directly back to the storeroom, where she had an old fabric-sample book. "Look—isn't this fabric in your quilt? And this one? And maybe this one?" Ruth excitedly pointed to five or six different fabrics.

"Maybe," Sarah responded. "I'm not as good as you are at remembering patterns, but they look familiar. Why do you ask?"

"Because the fabrics illustrated in this book were produced by a textile mill in England between 1810 and 1825 using cotton produced in this country. If these fabrics are in your quilt, that will help us to date it and prove its authenticity. Did you bring the quilt?"

"I did, but I locked it in the car. I wasn't sure what was on our agenda tonight."

"I'd love for us to talk about your quilt with the group tonight if you're willing," Ruth responded.

"I'd like that, too," Sarah replied, eager for an opportunity to share her treasure with her quilting friends.

Once everyone was congregated around the worktable, Ruth asked Sarah to tell the group about her exciting find.

Sarah proudly lifted the tote bag onto the table but didn't take the quilt out immediately. First, she talked about how she happened to find it and a little about what she'd learned so far. She then carefully removed the quilt and, with Ruth's help, spread it out on the table. Sarah stood back to watch their reaction.

"As hard as it will be," Ruth interjected, "please don't touch the quilt. It's extremely fragile, as you can see."

"This is spectacular," Delores muttered. "Just spectacular."

"Does it have a label?" Allison asked.

Ruth sighed and looked at Sarah. "No," Sarah responded. "But the quilter had embroidered what we think is the word *memories* on the back."

Delores, the oldest and most experienced member, was visibly awed by the quilt. "This is the oldest quilt I've seen outside of a museum. It's an incredible treasure, Sarah," she said, speaking barely above a whisper as if she'd been transported to the museum. "Too bad there's no label," she added.

"How old do you think it is?" Ruth asked Delores, hoping to confirm her own ideas.

"My guess would be at least 130 years old, probably even older," Delores responded. "I'd say this was probably made before the Civil War."

"That's exactly what I've been thinking." Pointing out the binding on the fourth side, Ruth expressed her idea that it might have originally been a bed quilt that was divided to make two cot quilts.

"What's a cot quilt?" Caitlyn, their youngest member, asked.

Sarah spoke up and explained the Sanitary Commission's request for long, narrow quilts for the soldiers' cots during the

Civil War. She refrained from mentioning that many soldiers were buried in their cot quilts, not wanting to detract from the excitement in the room. Several others had questions about the cot quilts but soon got back to examining Sarah's quilt more closely.

"What do you call this pattern?" Allison asked. Allison was a young mother and new to quilting.

"This is a very old pattern," Ruth responded. "It's called Grandmother's Flower Garden. These hexagon quilts started in England in the 1700s, but in the 1830s the pattern and directions for making it appeared in a newspaper in this country. It's been very popular since then."

"What makes it a flower garden?" Allison asked curiously.

"A Grandmother's Flower Garden has one hexagon in the middle, which is surrounded by six more in a circular fashion. Then there are another twelve hexagons around that row, forming a large colorful rosette."

"And you have a garden path running between them all," Delores added. She pulled a magazine out of her tote bag and opened it to a picture. "Like this one," she said, passing the magazine to Allison and pointing to the white hexagons between each complete flower.

"I love this quilt," Christina commented as she stood looking at it with her hands clasped behind her back. Kimberly smiled to herself, knowing that her sister was fighting the urge to touch the quilt. "It's just wonderful," Christina added.

"I don't see what's so good about it," Frank commented, frowning. Frank was a young man, mildly limited in his abilities, but with a keen interest in learning to quilt. He had been with the group since the day he saw a table runner in the window of Stitches that he wanted to make for his grandmother. Still frowning at the quilt, he added, "It's stained and all full of holes. It needs too much fixing."

Sarah noticed later during their refreshment break that Ruth's sister, Anna, spent time explaining to Frank about the respect quilters have for those who came before them and how they value the work that has survived. "That quilt could have been made by your great-great-great-grandmother," Sarah heard Anna say to him as his eyes grew wide with astonishment.

Earlier Ruth had copied a few pages from the sample book that she thought represented the style of fabrics used in Sarah's quilt and now passed them out to the group. "Do you think these are the kind of fabrics that were used in this quilt?" She went on to tell them about the sample book, which covered textiles produced during the first half of the nineteenth century.

"That fabric right there is on my paper," Frank called out immediately, pointing to one of the rosettes.

"It is?" Ruth asked, doubting that he was right. But when she looked more closely, she cried, "It is! You're absolutely right." Although the group was unable to find any other fabrics that were identical, they all agreed that they seemed very similar and were probably from the same period.

Sarah and Ruth carefully folded the quilt and returned it to the pillowcase Sarah had been using to transport her treasure. After a refreshment break, Delores asked if anyone would be interested in learning how to do traditional English paper piecing.

"What's that?" Caitlyn asked.

"That's probably the technique that was used to make Sarah's quilt. The technique came to this country from England in the late 1700s and was used by quilters to make hexagon quilts. It's done by hand, and you use a paper pattern that you baste the fabric to. Some of the very old ones used newspaper, but today you can buy precut papers and templates."

"It would take a long time to make a quilt that way," Sophie spoke up, "but I've been doing hand piecing, and it's very relaxing. We could make something small just to learn about it."

"Would you teach us, Sophie?" Allison asked.

"No," Sophie chuckled. "Not me. Delores is the expert in that area," she added, smiling at her mentor.

Delores said that she'd be happy to show the group the basics of paper piecing.

"We can schedule that for next week if you'd like," Ruth suggested, and everyone agreed.

"If it's alright with you," Delores said, speaking to the group, "I'd like to teach you how it was done back in the early 1800s—the traditional method. We can make something small using the original techniques, and then I'll show you some of the modern conveniences that make it faster and easier. I like to look at quilting in terms of its history. When I'm piecing or quilting by hand, like my great-grandmother did, it gives me a feeling of continuity and a connection to my past."

The group—particularly the older members—knew what Delores meant, and they agreed that they'd like for her to teach it that way.

"But you'll still show us the modern way, right?" young Caitlyn asked.

"I certainly will, and I'll give Ruth a list of items she can stock for the ones who want to go on with paper piecing beyond this class. Things like templates, temporary glue sticks, and even water-soluble foundation papers. But let's hold off on that until you know whether you're interested. For the time being," she added, turning to Ruth, "we'll just need template papers."

"I'll call the order in tomorrow," Ruth responded. "Okay, before we call it a night, does anyone have anything for show-and-tell?" Everyone began reaching for their projects eagerly.

It was Sarah's favorite time of the evening.

Chapter 6

"I'm sorry, ladies," the manager of the homeless shelter said as he flipped through the records. "There's nobody by that name listed here. People come and go, but we get them into the computer as they check in. There's no record for a Maud Templeton. My guess is that she's never made it here. Have you tried the private shelters?"

Sarah and Sophie were extremely disappointed. They had arrived before breakfast was served, hoping Maud would still be there. Charles had told them that the shelters generally insisted that everyone leave during the day. Turning to Sophie, Sarah said hopefully, "Well, this was just our first attempt. Let's move on to the list of church-run shelters that Charles found for us."

"Here's the list we hand out in case you don't have them all," the manager said, handing them a printed sheet.

"Thank you," Sarah said. "We appreciate your help." Looking down at the new list, Sarah saw that Charles had done an excellent job with his research. He had identified them all.

As they were walking out the door, the young man called to them. "Hold on. I wonder about this one. I have a

May Templeman. The kids that do the data entry make lots of mistakes. Yeah—I think this might be your lady."

"Is she here?" Sarah asked excitedly.

"Sorry, no. If this is your Maud Templeton, she was only here for a few weeks back three or four months ago. I remember her now. She insisted on paying us, which is unusual. We let folks stay here free for a while and charge a small fee later if they decide to stay on."

"She only stayed a few weeks?" Sarah asked. "Where did she go after that?"

"No idea. Some lady came and got her."

"Do you know who? Would her name be on that computer of yours?" Sophie asked.

The man shook his head. "No. Nothing there except their names and the dates they stayed. That's about it for our record keeping."

"Do you remember anything about the woman who picked her up?"

"Lady, that was months ago. Do you have any idea how many people come through these doors?"

"Sorry," Sarah replied contritely. "Thanks for your help."

"Who do you suppose picked up Maud?" Sophie asked after they left the shelter.

"We actually don't know that it was Maud that got picked up. I think we should continue to check out the other shelters."

There were only four on the list, but none had any record of a Maud Templeton. Three of the shelters were willing to check various spellings and dates, but the manager of the fourth one dismissed them, saying all of their people were regulars and known to him personally.

"Did you see those lines and lines of cots?" Sophie asked as they were driving toward home. "What must life be like for those people?"

"Very dismal, I would say," Sarah responded. "We take our homes for granted, but really we're very fortunate."

"So now what?" Sophie asked after a long pause while they both tried to imagine a different kind of life.

"I'm not sure what you'll think of this idea, but I believe we should try to see one of the grandsons."

"In prison?" Sophie gasped.

"We've done it before, Sophie. It was okay. Not the most pleasant way to spend an afternoon, but one or both of the boys just might know something. They might even be in touch with her."

Sophie seemed to be considering the idea before speaking. "Could you get Charles to find out where they are and why?"

"Sure. He'd do that for us. He'd even go with us if you'd be more comfortable."

"Let me think about that while you see what he can find out."

* * * * *

When Sarah pulled up in front of her house, it sounded as if she had pulled up to the town's animal shelter. Dogs were barking, yapping, whining, panting, and jumping up on the fence, each attempting to be the first to greet her. Sarah could count only four, but it seemed as if there were at least twice that number.

"What's going on?" she asked as she approached the fence and saw Charles using the hose to fill a children's swimming pool. The two larger dogs, Sophie's Emma and Sarah's

Barney, leaped into the pool, causing a wave that caught Charles by surprise. The two smaller dogs—Jennifer's little papillon, Blossom, and Caitlyn's dachshund, Sabrina—were looking on with trepidation.

"Where did that come from?" Sarah asked as she slipped through the gate while the dogs were distracted.

"It was Timothy's idea. He brought it over this morning along with Blossom and Emma."

"I hope he left a note for Sophie. I just dropped her off at home and when she finds her dog missing …"

At that moment, her cell phone rang. "There she is now." Sarah answered the phone by saying, "Your Emma is here, joyfully wallowing in the swimming pool that your son brought over." She went on to explain what was going on, and Sophie said she was on her way to join the fun.

Charles called to Sarah and asked her to call Andy and invite him to come on over. "Caitlyn and Penny are inside making devilled eggs, and Tim's on his way to the store for hot dogs and beer."

"I hope he brings rolls and sodas."

"Yes, I made him a list. Oh—Martha is also on her way as soon as she can get out of the office."

"So we're having a spontaneous pool party, huh? Shall I get my suit?" Sarah asked.

"Only if you want to swim with the dogs," Charles responded, totally drenched at that moment. Both Blossom and Sabrina had also jumped in, splashing water and causing a momentary scuffle among the four dogs.

"I am going in to change into something less susceptible to water damage," Sarah announced. "Send Sophie in if she gets here before I'm back."

When Sarah returned in a sundress, Charles had pulled the picnic table away from the pool and brought a folding table and a dozen folding chairs from the garage. "I thought we'd be more comfortable this way," he said. "The kids can have the picnic table." He also had opened the grill and was ready for the arrival of the hot dogs.

"I asked the girls what was in the Crock-Pot. They said they didn't know but that we were supposed to stay out of it. Whatever it is, it smells great."

"Tim brought that. He made chili for our hot dogs."

Before Sarah could respond about all that was going on in her kitchen, Caitlyn called out from the kitchen door. "Sarah, can Penny and I bake those cookies you have in the freezer?"

"Sure," she replied with resignation. Sarah sat down to watch the dogs, but her mind kept returning to all the things that needed to be done: dishes, silverware, napkins, and condiments. But as she was checking things off in her mind, it occurred to her that she should simply join the party and allow the others to take care of the details. It was hard for her to hold back, but she'd been trying to remind herself that every time she took on all the responsibility, she was robbing others of the opportunity to do something special for their friends.

Sarah pulled one of the extra chairs over and put her feet up. They'd been swelling lately, and she remembered that her mother's doctor had told her mother to put them up. Sarah had been trying to do it herself but knew she might need to see the doctor if this didn't work. Suddenly she realized that Martha had arrived while she was inside. Martha spotted her mother at the same moment and hurried over, giving her mother a gentle kiss on the cheek.

"Are you okay?" Martha asked, looking at her mother's swollen feet.

"I'm fine, just too much running around today." From across the yard, Timothy motioned for Martha, and she went to see what he wanted. They spoke for just a moment, and Sarah saw Martha nod her agreement and pull her cell phone out of her pocket. She spoke briefly to someone and glanced at her mother as she returned the phone to her pocket.

Something's up, Sarah thought.

"It's a party!" Sophie squealed as she burst through the gate, barely getting it closed before all four dogs could rush out in their excitement. Sophie sat down so they could all greet her without knocking her to the ground. The pool experience had wound them up. Emma, wanting to show off her new skill, ran toward the pool with Barney right behind her, both hitting the water simultaneously—again splashing Charles, who was now soaked and threatening to change into a bathing suit himself.

Sophie came across the yard and sat down next to Sarah. "So you didn't know this was happening?"

"No clue. It seemed to happen spontaneously once your son brought the pool and the dogs."

"Well, everyone seems to be having fun," Sophie commented. "Do you suppose my son bought enough hot dogs for this gang?"

"I'm trying to stay out of it, but just in case, I have two or three packages of kielbasa in the freezer. We can always put that on the grill."

Abruptly, all the dogs again ran to the side gate, barking and clawing. Tim and Martha hurried over to help the newcomers through the gate without losing any of the dogs. "Hi, Mom," Sarah's son called across all the ruckus, waving to his mother with one hand and holding little Alaina's hand with the other. His wife, Jennifer, was right behind him with the new baby in one arm and a grocery bag in the other.

"I know you folks prefer homemade," Jennifer called out apologetically to whoever could hear her, "but I only had fifteen minutes notice to get over here with my family and lots of potato salad."

"This is perfect," Charles said, taking the bag and calling to Caitlyn to come get it and put it in the refrigerator.

Sarah noticed that three-year-old Alaina, wearing her bathing suit, was heading straight for the pool. Little Blossom, being the smallest, joined her, probably feeling safer with her than the big dogs.

"Bring that grandson of mine over here," Sarah said, holding her arms out. Jonathan had been born in the early spring and, at three months, was a delightful, happy baby. He smiled up at his grandmother, and her heart melted.

A few hours later, the sun was setting, the dogs were curled up on a blanket with the girls, and the adults were relaxing around the fire Charles had built in their new patio firepit. "Since it's been such a lovely evening," Tim said reaching for Martha's hand, "and since the whole family is here and it just seems like the right thing to do, I'd like to ask a question."

"Sure," Charles casually responded, oblivious to what both Sarah and Sophie immediately realized was about to happen.

"Martha Miller," Timothy began, "will you marry me?" With a slight tug on the hand he was still holding, he guided her into his arms as they both stood.

"Timothy Ward, I'd be pleased to marry you," she responded, looking over his shoulder at her mother and smiling. After tearful embracing, laughter, and hand shaking, Charles slipped into the kitchen and returned with a package of plastic glasses and the bottle of champagne he'd been saving for exactly this occasion.

Plastic? Sarah thought but didn't say.

As Penny was preparing to leave with her father and Martha, Sarah took her aside and said, "You didn't look surprised."

"I wasn't. Dad told me what he was going to do. I said it was a good idea."

Sarah smiled. "I agree," she responded. "A very good idea."

Chapter 7

"Are you happy about our kids?" Sarah asked as she and Sophie drove toward Hamilton and the maximum-security prison.

"Ecstatic," she replied. "My son couldn't have found a better wife. Martha brings out the best in my son."

"Well, I think your son is already the best, and I'm delighted that my daughter realizes that. You know, she's been overcautious since her marriage to Greyson."

"He was a terrible man. Timmy told me he was back in prison."

"Where he belongs, and far from here."

"What was Charles able to find out about Maud's grandsons?"

"Well, like I told you yesterday, Jerome is the only one in a prison near us. His brother is in jail in Texas for some minor drug charge."

"And Jerome is serving time for murder, you told me, but you didn't have any details at the time."

"I still don't. Charles is going to the courthouse today to read the transcripts of his trial."

"What if he's dangerous?" Sophie asked, sounding uneasy.

"We'll be perfectly safe, Sophie. Remember when we visited Andy?"

"Yes, I remember, and we were right in the room with him. He could have strangled us at any time."

"Now that's not true. There was a guard in the room, too."

"True."

"Charles said we'd be at a bulletproof window and talking to Jerome on a phone. We'll be fine," Sarah added confidently.

"If you say so …"

After turning over their purses and watching while the guard placed them in lockers, the two friends waited for an escort to take them to meet with Maud's grandson. They were both getting nervous—Sophie because she watched too much television and Sarah because she feared this would be another dead end.

The guard escorted them up to a booth and pulled a second chair over for Sophie. The chair opposite them on the other side of the glass was empty. After a few minutes, another guard brought a tough-looking man in and set him in the empty chair across from Sarah and Sophie. Sophie scooted her chair back a few inches. The man appeared older than Sarah had expected. He didn't make eye contact with them. Sarah picked up the receiver and motioned for the man to do the same. He reluctantly did.

"What you white bitches want with me?" he growled, still not looking at either woman.

"We're here about your grandmother, Maud Templeton."

"She croak?" he asked without emotion.

"No. Well, not to our knowledge. Actually, we're trying to locate her and hoped you could help."

With a sarcastic smirk, he responded, "So go knock on her door. She's in the phone book."

Sarah explained about the housing development being torn down and what little she knew about Maud after that time. "She was in a shelter for a few weeks, but we've lost track of her after that." The man showed no interest. "Has she been here to see you?" Sarah asked.

"Yeah," he grunted.

Feeling a degree of hope, Sarah asked, "When was she here?"

"Few years back," he muttered, still showing no interest. But then he asked why they wanted to find her.

"We want to make sure she's not on the street. If she needs a place to stay, her caseworker may have something for her. We were hoping you could help us find her, but I guess you can't."

"You got it right," Jerome said with a snicker as he hung up the phone, stood, and yelled for the guard, saying, "We're through here."

"Wait," Sophie hollered, loud enough for him to hear her without the phone. He turned and glared at her. "Please wait," she mouthed. Taking the phone from Sarah, she motioned for him to pick his up. "Someone came for her and took her out of the shelter," she said. "It was probably a friend. Do you have any idea who that might have been?"

Jerome appeared to be thinking about Sophie's question but didn't respond. When he finally did, he just said, "It's time for grub," and walked over to the door, turning his back on the women.

"Well that was a total bust," Sophie said as the guard escorted them through the front gate.

"Yeah," Sarah responded despondently.

"So what next?"

Sarah didn't answer right away but finally shook her head slowly and responded, "I have absolutely no idea."

* * * * *

Over coffee the next morning, Charles said, "Well, I guess we have a wedding to plan."

"I don't know how much help Martha will want from us. You know how independent she is, but when she comes to lunch tomorrow, we'll talk about it. I've been picturing Pastor John's sanctuary all decorated with flowers …"

At that moment, the phone rang.

"Good morning, Sophie. You're up early."

"I had an idea."

"Tell me," Sarah responded eagerly.

"Well, last night I took out all my 3″ by 5″ cards. I have a couple dozen with notes, you know." Sarah tried to imagine what her friend could possibly have written on her cards since they were for clues and, as far as she could see, they didn't have any. "So I shuffled them and spread them out, and I could immediately see what we should do next."

"And what's that?" Sarah asked, trying to keep the amusement out of her voice.

"We need to talk to Darnell."

"Who's Darnell?" Charles mouthed. Sarah had the phone on speaker so she could finish her breakfast while they talked.

"The other grandson," she said.

"What?" Sophie asked.

"Sorry, Sophie. I was talking to Charles."

"Well, talk to me! Let's go to Texas."

"Sophie, we're not going to Texas. But let me see if Charles can help. Maybe he can arrange for us to talk to Darnell by phone."

"If he's anything like his brother, he'll just hang up."

"True, but let's give it a try."

"By the way," Charles interjected, "I wish I'd known about your 3″ by 5″ card trick when I was still with the police department."

"It's a great way to solve crimes," Sophie responded proudly. "I'll show you how I do it sometime."

"Thanks, Sophie," he replied with a chuckle.

As it turned out, Sophie's suggestion worked. Later that afternoon, Sarah was on the phone with Darnell, who proved to be much more cooperative than his brother. "I'll be out of here in a month," Darnell offered at the end of their conversation, "and I'll come help you look for her. I miss Granny. She was always good to us."

Sarah called Sophie the minute she hung up to give her the news. "We have the woman's name, Sophie. Darnell remembered her. He said his grandmother had this good friend over the years that he was sure would have taken her in if she needed a place to stay. He said this woman, Bertha Washington, lived with them for a few years after her husband died."

"How will we find her?"

"Charles already has. She lives over on the east side. It's not a great area, and he wants to go with us when we go to see her."

"See? My detecting cards worked," Sophie said proudly. "When do we leave?"

"How about tomorrow morning? Martha's coming for lunch today."

"Tim didn't mention that," Sophie responded, sounding hurt.

"No, it's just Martha. We're having mother-daughter time. Charles and Timothy are going to the computer show."

"Okay. Tomorrow morning, then. I'll be ready."

* * * * *

"This is a pretty fancy lunch, Mother. What's the occasion?" She looked at her mother with a tilted head, but Sarah could see her daughter's lips quivering as she fought to hold back a smile.

She seems very happy, Sarah thought. "We're celebrating a beautiful new beginning," she said. "And hopefully we'll be making some plans."

"I knew it," Martha responded. "You and Sophie have had your heads together, haven't you? Tim said Sophie probably had all the details worked out, and we haven't even set a date."

"Actually, honey, Sophie and I have agreed to stay out of the planning totally, except for anything you ask us to do. And we're both happy to help in any way if that's what you want. I just want this to be your day, and I want you to have whatever kind of wedding you'd like to have."

"Thank you, Mom," she responded gratefully. "Tim and I both appreciate that. We've talked about it, and we both want the same thing."

"And that is?"

"A small wedding, just the family and a few close friends, at Pastor John's church with a simple luncheon right here in your backyard."

"Oh, Martha, that would be wonderful. I could make ..."

"No. That's the other part. I want to have it catered. I want to have you available to me—I'll be a wreck, and besides, I want you to be able to enjoy the party."

Sarah wanted to object. She wanted to do it all herself, but she had to ask herself why. *Martha wants to do this, and I'm not going to take it over.* "That sounds lovely, honey. What time of the year are you thinking of?"

"Early September," her daughter responded. "While it's still warm."

Sarah knew one thing she could do starting right away that her daughter couldn't object to. She'd begin planning the garden so it would look spectacular by September. Martha would never get suspicious since she knew how much her mother loved gardening. Her dahlias would still be in bloom, she thought, and perhaps she'd add a colorful array of asters. She would talk to the people at the nursery and get any other ideas they might have. She also knew that if she took very good care of her roses throughout the summer, they would look stunning in September. She had planted the climbing variety the first year they were in the house, and the vines were eagerly scrambling up the fence on all three sides of the backyard.

"You look deep in thought, Mother, and I know that look. What are you up to?"

"Oh nothing, dear. Just picturing you in a wedding gown."

"No wedding gown. I want a nice suit."

"Silk?" her mother suggested in the form of a question.

Martha laughed. "Okay, silk, and you can help me pick it out."

Sarah smiled and nodded her agreement. "And maybe a pretty dress for the garden party?"

"Okay," Martha chuckled. "A silk suit and maybe a pretty dress …"

"And my treat."

"Mother, I work. I can afford …"

"No argument. It's my right to buy my daughter's wedding dress. But you get to pick it out."

"Deal," Martha agreed, scooping out another helping of pasta salad. "But that's it."

"You need to talk to Pastor John and set a date."

"I know, Mom," Martha responded in a tone that gently reminded Sarah to leave the details to her daughter. "We're seeing him after services on Sunday. I'm still a member, and Tim wants to join the church. I've always loved Pastor John, and now he's become a part of our lives. We want to keep it that way."

Sarah smiled, knowing that her daughter was well on her way to a far happier life. Martha was a prominent scientist, and her last twenty years had been spent immersed in her work. Sarah was glad to see her emerging into life outside her lab.

"When shall we go shopping?" Martha asked casually.

"How about you take a couple of days off from work, and we drive up to Chicago? There are these lovely lakeside shops, and we could spend the night at the Lakefront Hotel. Oh, and there's the honeymoon wardrobe to think about, too."

Martha threw her head back and laughed, shaking her head with exasperation. "You just aren't going to keep this simple, are you?"

"I'm trying," Sarah responded contritely. "I haven't tried to plan the menu."

"Not yet ..." Martha said, knowing her mother too well.

Chapter 8

"That's our turn right up there," Sarah announced, pointing to an intersecting road.

"I know, dear," Charles responded. "I'm following the GPS."

"And it's probably in the next block, since these are the 400s and the numbers are going up," she added. Charles nodded his head but didn't respond.

"That's it right up there," Sophie hollered from the back seat. "See? It's green just like Darnell remembered."

Charles sighed and pulled up in front of the house just as his GPS announced their arrival at their destination. "Don't know how I'd make it without you gals," he said with that sarcastic tone Sarah really didn't like but tolerated.

The neighborhood didn't look as bad as Charles had remembered when he was a cop. He knew there had been efforts in the past few years to close down most of the crack houses on the east side. Driving into the neighborhood, he had noticed an apartment building for senior citizens under construction. A block later, children were enjoying a new playground. *All part of the city's revitalization program*, he told himself. He'd never been too impressed by the city's efforts in the past. It seemed to result in more crime and more people on the street. *Appears to be working better this time*, he thought.

"Do you want me to go in with you?" he asked as the women were getting out of the car.

"It might be better if Sophie and I go in alone and talk to Maud. But keep your phone handy. I'll call if we need you."

The house was in need of fresh paint but otherwise appeared to be well cared for. Foundation plantings were overgrown, but the grass was mowed, and there were flowers in pots on the porch. The door was opened moments after Sarah knocked. The elderly woman appeared puzzled but was polite. "Can I help you?" she asked.

"I'm Sarah Parker, and this is my friend Sophie Ward. Are you Bertha Washington?"

"I am. What can I do for you ladies?" she repeated.

"We're looking for Maud Templeton, and her grandson said you might know where she is."

"Not Jerome, I hope. Maud doesn't want anything to do with him."

"Actually, it was Darnell who suggested we talk to you. He said you and Maud had been close friends."

"Still are," Bertha said as she opened the screen door and invited them in. "Who's that man in the car?" she asked suspiciously.

"That's my husband. He just drove us here."

"It's hot out there. Have him come in. I was just fixing iced tea." Sarah stepped back out and motioned for Charles to come in. He hurried to the door, looking worried.

"What's wrong?" he whispered, expecting trouble.

"Nothing. Ms. Washington just wanted you to come in out of the heat."

"So is Maud here?" he asked as they went in.

"I don't know yet. We'll get to that." She supposed it was his police interrogation background, but he always wanted to get to the point. He wasn't much for the gracious art of preliminary small talk. "Just follow my lead," she added.

Once all four were settled on the well-worn upholstered furniture in the sitting room, Bertha was the first to mention Maud. "Well, I guess you already know that I took Maud out of that terrible shelter a few months ago and brought her here to live with me."

"That was kind of you, Ms. Washington …" Sarah was saying, but Bertha interrupted her.

"Didn't do it to be kind. Maud and I are like sisters. Besides, she took me in after Bernie died."

"Your husband?" Sophie asked, wanting to be involved in the conversation.

"Been gone twenty-five years now, God bless his soul."

Charles sat through another ten minutes of what he thought to be unnecessary chatter. He tried to appear patient and sipped his tea, but ultimately, he could take it no longer. "Does Maud Templeton still live here?" he asked, and Sarah frowned at him.

"Mercy, yes," Bertha responded. "Been here every day for three months …"

"May we see her?"

"… except today," Bertha continued. "Today she went on the medical bus to the foot doctor. Her bunions."

"Do you know when she'll be back?"

"Should be any minute now. She's been gone three or four hours. More tea?"

Charles sighed deeply, but only Sarah seemed to notice.

"What do you want with Maud anyway?" Bertha asked. Sarah was relieved to have a topic of conversation introduced to keep them occupied while they waited for Maud. She told Bertha about the quilt, probably even more than the woman wanted to know. Finally, they heard the front door open, and a wispy, petite woman limped into the room.

"Bertha, who are all these white folks?"

"They're here to see you, Maud. They want to ask you about an old quilt that was up in the attic of your old place. Someone found it when they were tearing it down."

"Laudamercy," Maud exclaimed. "I haven't thought about Mama's quilt for years."

"It was your mother's?" Sarah asked, sadly realizing she would have to return *Memories* to this woman.

"Not really hers. It was actually the boys that found it."

"*Stole* it is more like it," Sarah heard Bertha mutter under her breath.

"Could you start from the beginning?" Sarah's very impatient husband said. "Where did the quilt originally come from?"

"Don't know that, sir. Don't have any idea. The boys just brought it in one night along with a lot of smelly stuff that was covered with soot, like it'd been in a fire. I heard there'd been a house fire over on Nineteenth Street that night, and, looking back and knowing those boys better now, they probably robbed the place. Back then I never would have thought that. I figured they were good boys. Both in jail now, one for murder. I should have known they was no good."

"So they brought the quilt to you?"

"They took everything except the quilt to the junk man. I kept the quilt. They brought me back three dollars and told me that was all they got. Don't believe that neither. Anyway, I took it upstairs to cover Mama, but she only used it a few weeks. She'd been terrible sick and just laid in the bed. Wouldn't even eat when I tried to feed her. One day she just gave up and went to live with the Lord. I kept the quilt folded up on her bed for a few days, but Jerome was threatening to take over her room, so I wrapped the quilt and put it in the attic so he couldn't sell it. There was something special about that old quilt. I never knew just what, but I knew it should be protected from my boys."

Everyone sat quietly for a few moments, contemplating what Maud had said. "So how did you come by the quilt?" Maud asked Sarah.

Sarah told her about seeing it in a thrift shop and buying it. "But if you want it back, Maud, I'll bring it to you. It's really yours."

"Not mine," she responded. "It belonged to whoever's house burnt down."

Charles wondered if he could find out about that fire, but he'd need more information. He helped Maud reconstruct the time frame, which she couldn't pin down any closer than to say, "Jerome's in his forties now, and I think he was nine or ten when he brought that stuff home." Charles did some quick calculations and came up with the mid-80s.

"And you say it was over on Nineteenth Street?"

"That's what I remember the boys saying."

"I know you raised your grandsons," Sarah said, having learned that earlier from Bertha. "But what happened to their mother?"

"Her rotten husband killed my Clarissa," Maud stated with conviction.

Sarah and Sophie gasped, "He killed her?"

"Maud," Bertha scolded. "You know that's not what happened."

"Sure as I'm sitting here. I knew it the minute the police came to tell me she was gone. My girl was always bruised up and had black eyes. She'd always have some crazy story about how it happened, but I could tell that she was just covering for him."

"You told the police about your suspicions?" Charles asked.

"Sure did, but they just kept saying it was drugs."

"The police didn't believe you?" Charles asked, trying to remember the case, but it was probably before he made detective.

"Oh, Jamal could be a charmer when he wanted to be. He had those cops wrapped around his finger. He convinced them my girl was no good. He told them she drank, abused the boys, took drugs, and whatever else he could think of, but none of that was true."

"Maud, now you know …" Bertha began to object, but Maud interrupted her.

"Okay, so she drank a little, but who wouldn't being married to that man?" she responded defensively.

"How did you get the boys away from their father?" Sophie asked.

"Oh, that was the easy part. He didn't want them. He drove over here right after the funeral and dumped Jerome and Darnell off, and I haven't seen that man since. I don't know where he is and sure don't care. Neither do the boys, for that matter."

"I thought there were three boys. What happened to the third?"

"Jackson? I don't know. He was the oldest, and Clarissa wasn't his mother. Jamal already had him when he met my girl. I asked Jamal why he didn't bring all three of the boys, and he just sneered. Jackson might be dead, too, for all I know."

Bertha shook her head and rolled her eyes but didn't say anything.

Before they left, Sarah again asked Maud if she wanted the quilt and Maud repeated, "Not mine to have. You paid money for it, so it's yours now. Pleased to meet you folks," she added, turned her back, and limped out of the room.

Bertha walked them to the door and said, "You'll have to excuse Maud. She always had a blind eye when it came to that girl of hers."

The three friends were quiet on the drive home. It had been a day filled with emotion, leaving Sarah and Sophie feeling wrung out. Charles, however, was making plans for finding out about the fire, learning who was living in the house at the time, and checking out this Jamal character. *Once a cop, always a cop*, he often told himself.

Chapter 9

"I'm off to meet with the fire chief," Charles announced as he came through the kitchen heading for the garage door.

"Do you think they have information going back that far?"

"With computers, they probably have it easily accessible. If not, I may spend the day going through file boxes." Which was exactly what he ended up doing.

Chief Deegan met Charles in the reception area, shook his hand firmly, and greeted him with a thick Irish brogue. "Glad to see you again, Detective. How can we help you?"

"I'm a civilian now, Deeg. I retired a few years back."

"Surprised to hear that, Charlie. You seemed to love the work."

"I did, but you know this old ticker told me it was time."

"Sorry," his friend replied. "Anyway, how can we help you?"

"I'm trying to help my wife solve a problem. She's trying to find out something about a quilt that was rescued from a fire back in the mid-1980s over on Nineteenth Street. I was hoping you could help me find out who was living in the house."

"That's not much to go on, Charlie. If we'd been on the computer in those days, maybe—but we weren't. The city didn't vote computers into our budget until the late 1990s."

"What kind of records do you have from the 1980s?" Charles asked.

"Paper records. That's it, Charlie. We've got boxes and boxes of paper in storage, but I don't have the manpower to go through it."

"Could I take a shot at it?" Charles asked, and Chief Deegan laughed.

"Let me show you something." As they walked through the administrative offices, the chief called to his assistant and said, "We're heading out to the annex. Call if you need me," he added as he patted the shirt pocket where he kept his cell phone.

Chief Deegan led Charles across the room and into what appeared to be a living room and kitchen combination. "This is our residential area: the day room and, through that door over there, you can see the cots. Our guys are ready to hit the road at a moment's notice."

"Impressive," Charles replied, noting the modern conveniences in the kitchen area.

They walked through another doorway that placed them immediately into the large apparatus bay, where the fire-fighting and emergency-response vehicles were lodged. "Over there's bay support and vehicle maintenance. The men's gear is in that room we just passed between residential and the bay."

"Where are we headed?"

"Out back to the annex. We keep all our records out there—at least the ones that aren't on the computer. What a time-saver that crazy machine has been, at least once we learned how to use it."

The annex turned out to be a large Quonset hut behind the station and not visible from the street. "Haven't seen one of these for some time," Charles remarked.

"I know. They've been promising us a building for years, but now they're saying we might not need one. There's talk of having a crew come in and enter all this stuff on a database."

"What a job!"

"You aren't kidding. This station goes back into the 60s." Chief Deegan unlocked the door, and Charles was stunned by the sheer volume of boxes stacked on shelf after shelf. "See what I mean? I can't see you finding what you're looking for on your own."

"I agree, but I think I can get some help. Could I come back this afternoon with a couple of guys?"

"You sure can, Charlie. I owe you, anyway. Remember that jam you got my kid out of some years back?"

"Ah," Charles responded with a spark of recognition. "Your son Liam, right?"

"Right, and that boy's been on the straight and narrow ever since. That must have been some lecture you gave him that night."

"It wasn't so much the lecture, Deeg. I put him in the tank with some real scumbags and let him think he was there for the night. I told the officer to stay close by and make sure he didn't get hurt. I just wanted to scare the bejesus out of him."

"Well you sure did. You know he went on to trade school? He's working over in Hamilton at the airport. Diesel mechanic now."

"Glad to hear it, Chief."

"How about your boys?"

"Both out in Colorado now. One's into law, the other's a teacher."

"They finally grow up, don't they?"

"Most of them," Charles responded, thinking about Maud's grandsons.

As they walked back through the station, Chief Deegan said a little regretfully that he'd hoped his son would follow him into the department. "You know I'm third generation. My father and grandfather were both with the fire brigade over in County Clare."

"Where's that?" Charles asked, looking puzzled.

"West coast of Ireland. That's where I was born. Came here when I'd just turned twenty. Married Iona and brought her with me. The family thought I was leaving the tradition, but I surprised them. Been with this department since 1974."

"Over forty years," Charles marveled. "Any thoughts of retiring?"

"I'd planned to last year, but Iona got sick and the medical bills began to pile up. I figured I might as well stay on. I don't go out on the trucks anymore. Way too old and stiff for that, but the desk job suits me."

Thinking about his friend being on the job through the 1980s, he said, "Maybe when I find the paperwork, it'll trigger a memory for you. You just might have worked the fire."

"Maybe. But after all these years, it's not likely I'll remember one specific fire. Anyway, good luck to you. I'll leave the key with Kenny. He's in the office today."

"Thanks, Chief. I appreciate your help.

"Take care, Charlie," and the chief headed toward his office.

Once Charles was in the car, he put calls into Timothy and Andy. Both men agreed to help him that afternoon.

"There's no reason Sophie and I can't help, too," Sarah complained as she made toast for their BLTs.

"We'd be stepping all over each other, honey. The shelves are close, the boxes are heavy, and there are no tables, so we'll probably be sorting on the floor." The more he talked, the less attractive it sounded.

"Okay, but call me when you come up with something."

"I'll do better than that. I'll rush right home with whatever I find, and you can call Sophie to join us. She can make 3″ by 5″ cards," he added with a mocking grin.

"Don't make fun of my friend," Sarah responding, attempting to look irritated.

Later she walked him out to the car and kissed him on the cheek. "Thank you for helping me with this, dear. This is above and beyond …"

"Nothing is above or beyond as far as I'm concerned." He blew her a kiss and backed out of the driveway.

* * * * *

While Charles was gone, Sarah took advantage of the quiet time to finish Jimmy's sports quilt. All she had left was to add the borders: a thin black inner border and a wider one that she planned to cut from the rock fabric Sophie had found. Standing back and looking at the fabric lying against the completed top, however, she frowned.

"I just don't like that fabric," she said aloud. She rummaged through her stash and found a piece of navy tone-on-tone she had intended to use on a charity project later in the year. She laid that and a thin red strip against the completed top and said, "Now that's much better."

By the time Charles returned, she had completed the quilt and had called Christina to schedule having it quilted on her long-arm quilting machine.

"Good news," she announced as he walked into the house. "I finished Jimmy's quilt."

"Better news," Charles responded. "I have the name of the owner of the house that burned down."

As she again saw the *Memories* quilt slipping from her hands, Sarah felt a wave of sadness. She attempted to hide it from her husband as she smiled her appreciation.

Chapter 10

"I found this fantastic dress … I know I said I wanted a suit, but I saw this in the window of Crystal's, and it's just perfect … It's silk like you wanted, and it's very flattering, and I know you'll just love it."

Sarah had answered the phone before she had her first cup of coffee. For a moment, she wasn't sure who was on the other end of the line. Martha was excitedly chattering in a manner unlike the daughter Sarah had known for forty-some years. "It has this perfect neckline," Martha continued, "and the sleeves—oh, the sleeves—you've got to see it. So can you?"

"Can I what, sweetheart?"

"Can you go with me today to look at it? I just know you'll love it."

"Honey, if you love it, I know I will. The dress you get married in should be perfect in your eyes, and it sure sounds like this one is. Let me check with Charles and see if we can move a few things around …"

"Oh, Mom, don't do that. This can wait," her daughter said, trying to hide her disappointment.

"I don't think it can wait, Martha," Sarah responded with compassion. "It sounds to me like this is something that needs doing right now. Hold on just a minute."

Sarah hurried down the hall to Charles' computer room, where he was already attempting to track down the owner of the house on Nineteenth. "Charles," she said as he looked up, holding his hands in the air ready to hit the next keys. "I'm sorry to interrupt you, but Martha's on the line. She would really love for me to go look at a dress she's considering. Would you mind if I slip out for a few hours? I know we were planning to start this search right away this morning ..."

"It's no problem. In fact, I'll probably be working on the computer all morning. I have a number of sites to look at, and I also want to sign into the criminal justice database and poke around there for some information."

"You think the owner of the house is a criminal?" Sarah asked, somewhat stunned.

"No. I want to get more information on this Jamal character, since Maud thinks he killed her daughter."

"Charles, don't go there. That was more than thirty years ago. I want to talk to the owner of that house and see where they got the quilt."

"I know, and I'll have what we need by the time you get back. Go on with Martha now, and we'll talk about what I find out when you get home."

Sarah went back to the kitchen, poured herself a cup of coffee, and picked up the phone. "He said we should go ahead and go. He's working on the computer now and doesn't need me."

"What's going on, anyway?" Martha asked.

"We're just attempting to track down some history on that old quilt I bought. That can wait. Are you really free to go this morning?" Sarah asked, surprised that her daughter would be taking off work for any reason.

"That's exactly what I was hoping we could do. I'm afraid someone will buy it, and there's only one in my size. I'll come pick you up. Can you be ready in a half-hour?"

"Martha, the stores don't open until 10:00. Come on over and have some breakfast with us, and we'll leave in time to be the first ones in the store. Okay?"

"Okay, Mom."

Sarah chopped green peppers and onions and pulled the container of leftover ham out of the refrigerator. By the time Martha arrived, Sarah had western omelets waiting in the warming oven, along with a pan of biscuits. Charles was pouring orange juice and coffee for three.

"So tell me, Charles, how are you planning to find out where this quilt came from?" Martha asked once they were seated at the table.

Charles and Sarah caught her up on everything they had done so far and told her about locating the original fire department's report.

"Tim filled me in on that search," Martha said, shaking her head. "All those boxes."

"It was quite a job, but from that report I was able to get the name of the owner at the time of the fire." Turning to Sarah, he added, "And this is the part you don't know yet. Unfortunately, the house was sold as soon as it was reconstructed, and I haven't been able to locate the original owner."

"And the people that bought it?" Martha asked.

"They still live there, but there's no reason they'd know anything about the quilt."

"This is discouraging," Sarah said, laying her fork down and taking a sip of her coffee.

"Not so much. I'm on the original owner's trail. His name is Benjamin Bentz. He'd be seventy-three years old now, and I can probably track him down through the social security records."

"You have access to those records?" Martha asked, looking surprised.

"I have access to people who have access ..." Charles replied with a sly grin.

"So you do," Martha chuckled. "Mom, let's get moving. The stores open in forty minutes."

"And they are fifteen minutes from here, my dear. Pour yourself another cup of coffee and I'll finish dressing."

"I'll clean up," Charles offered, noticing that Sarah had already cleaned up her cooking mess and all that was required was to place their dishes in the dishwasher.

"Thank you," Sarah called over her shoulder as she headed for the master bedroom.

* * * * *

"Sophie, can you come over and bring your 3″ by 5″ cards? Charles has some information for us."

"I'll be right there. But where have you been all morning? I've been calling, and I kept getting the machine."

"Charles must have been on the phone. Martha wanted me to go look at a dress this morning that she's considering for the wedding."

"A wedding gown?" Sophie crooned. "How exciting."

"No. Remember, she doesn't want a gown. She originally wanted a suit, but she saw this dress and fell in love with it."

"What's it like?"

"She left it here for me to show you. She has it on approval, but I'm sure she'll keep it. Come on over."

Turning to her husband, Sarah said, "Sophie's on her way. Are you going to tell me what you learned while I was gone?"

"Not until Sophie gets here," he responded. "I want to answer all the questions at once."

Fifteen minutes later, the kitchen door flew open and Sophie came in breathless from rushing. "I saw the garage door open and decided to take the shortcut right into the kitchen," she announced. "So what's going on?" She pulled out a chair and tossed her pack of 3″ by 5″ cards down on the table. "Okay if I pour a cup?" she asked, pointing toward the coffeepot.

"I'll do that," Sarah offered. "Go ahead and sit down. Charles is eager to tell us what he's found."

"Okay," Charles began. He started by filling in Sophie the parts that Sarah already knew, primarily his trip to the fire department and the massive search through the old files.

"Timmy told me," Sophie responded. "He said there wasn't much order to the way stuff was filed and that you boys had a time digging through all those dusty old records."

"We did, but I couldn't have done it without your son and Andy. We worked out a system and literally flew through the job. Within a few hours, we had the boxes narrowed down to the ones from the 1980s, and just about the time the supervisor was ready to throw us out for the night, we found the fire on Nineteenth Street."

"How did you know it was the right one?" Sophie asked.

"There was a police report attached about it being looted that night and nothing of value being left in the house. Had to be the right one. But just to make sure, I called my old supervisor at the police department this morning and asked him to check their records. It was the only report they had of a looting on Nineteenth Street during that time period. There were robberies in that district, but none of them also involved the fire department. I'm sure this is our crime scene."

Sarah smiled to herself. She enjoyed seeing her husband so easily fall into his old habits. She knew he missed being a detective.

"Hold on. I want to make some notes," Sophie announced. While Sarah freshened up their coffee and added a plate of cookies to the table, Sophie jotted down a few words on each of five or six cards. Charles wondered what she was writing but decided not to ask.

"So," she said when she looked up. "Go on."

"So I got the name of the owner, Benjamin Bentz."

"Spell that," and Sophie grabbed another card. "Shall we go see this Benjamin Bentz guy?" she asked once she got his name on the card.

"Unfortunately, he isn't there anymore. He sold the house after making the needed repairs and moved down to Kentucky."

"And?" Sarah was beginning to look worried.

"And I spoke to him this morning," Charles added.

Sophie clapped with excitement. "We're on the trail of the quilt."

"Not so fast," Charles said, looking reluctant to continue.

"Surely he must know where he got the quilt?" Sarah asked dubiously.

"He doesn't know a thing about the quilt. He never lived in the house. It was rented by a family who had just moved into town back in the 70s. He said they were clearly down on their luck, and he lowered the rent for the first few years until they got on their feet. They lived there for fifteen years, from 1970 until the fire in 1985."

"And then the fire ..." Sarah added sympathetically.

"He said they lost everything the night of the fire. What didn't burn up was stolen during the night. He said it was heartbreaking to talk with them, but there just wasn't anything else he could do for them. He said he'd been sick himself and had moved to Kentucky to be near his daughters."

"But he knows where these people are, right?" Sophie asked hopefully.

"Sorry. No. But he gave me all their names."

"What do you mean all their names?" Sarah asked.

"Well, that was thirty years ago. The kids are grown now, and Benjamin remembers them all. We have the parents' names now and all of the children. Their name is Anderson: Susan and Philip are the parents; there are two sons, Richard and Paul; and there's a daughter, Sadie. She might be married, but I might be able to track her down as well."

"This sounds like a monumental task," Sophie sighed.

"Not with the computer it isn't," Charles said confidently.

"And definitely not if you were ever a cop," Sarah added, smiling at her husband.

"I'm taking a break and heading over to the gym," Charles announced as he stood up. "What are you gals up to this afternoon?"

"We have a dress to discuss," Sophie announced as she swiped her scattered cards into a neat pile.

Once Charles was out the door, the two friends headed to the sewing room, where Sarah had hung the dress. She carefully unzipped the dress bag and lifted the dress out.

Sophie gasped and said, "Oh, Sarah, this will look stunning on your daughter."

"It does," Sarah responded, gently lifting the fabric so Sophie could see the subtle tone-on-tone pattern. "When Martha stepped out of the dressing room in this dress, she took my breath away." The dress was silk jacquard in a soft buttercream color with a barely visible variegated floral pattern woven into the fabric. The scooped neckline and A-line silhouette gave the dress a subtle feminine touch.

"I love this dress, Sarah. It's simple but elegant. She will look beautiful at the church, and yet it's understated enough for the garden party."

"I love it, too, and so does Martha. You should see it with her beautiful olive complexion."

"I've always wanted to ask you about that. With her dark hair and olive skin, she looks almost Mediterranean—not at all like you."

"She doesn't look much like her father, either, but his mother had that same striking beauty. Her people were from the south of France. I have a picture of her around her somewhere. She was a beautiful woman."

"So is Martha," Sophie commented, "And she'll look fantastic in this dress."

They put the dress back into the bag and spent some time talking about how Jimmy's sports quilt should be quilted. "I think I'm just going to leave it up to Christina and her sister. They're very creative." Kimberly and Christina had been doing most of the quilting for the members of their quilt club since buying their long-arm quilting machine.

"I'm going home," Sophie announced, "but call me if you and Charles make any headway this afternoon."

"I will. I'm hoping we find at least one person from that family that still lives in town."

Chapter 11

"I found him." Charles announced proudly.

"Benjamin Bentz? You found him yesterday. Oh, you mean you found one of the renters—the Andersons?"

"No …"

"Then exactly who *did* you find, Charles?" Sarah asked, sounding a bit annoyed.

"Jamal Davis, Maud's son-in-law."

"Charles! Why are you wasting time on this?"

"I'm not so sure it's wasted. Just wait until I tell you where I found him."

"Okay," Sarah sighed with resignation. "Where did you find him?"

"Jamal Davis is listed as the surviving spouse of a thirty-nine-year-old woman in New Orleans."

Sarah looked up abruptly. "Surviving spouse? Another wife is dead? Has he been arrested?" she asked.

"Yes, another wife is dead, and, no, he hasn't been arrested. I read about the wife's death in their local paper, and it's reported as accidental."

"Again?" Sarah knew that Maud Templeton suspected Jamal of killing her daughter many years ago, and maybe she wasn't so far off. But Sarah hoped Charles wasn't planning to get involved in the investigation. His medications had recently been increased, and the doctor had emphasized the importance of limiting stress. She knew he enjoyed the challenges, but she didn't want him getting involved in another murder investigation. "What are you thinking of doing, Charles?" she asked.

"I think I should call the investigating officer and put him in touch with Maud. It might help both of them."

"I agree," she responded with a sigh of relief. "I'm just glad you aren't planning to try to solve the crimes yourself, but I'd like to go see Maud and tell her in person before the police contact her."

"I'll drive over with you as soon as I get dressed," Charles said. He was still in his pajamas since he'd gone straight to the computer early that morning, eager to start the search for members of the Anderson family. Being a common name, he knew this would be a challenging search since the only address he had was thirty years old. It was only by chance that he ran the name Jamal Davis before he looked for the Andersons.

"Give me a few minutes to give Louisiana a call first."

* * * * *

That evening as Sarah and Sophie were driving to the quilt shop for Delores' English paper-piecing class, they talked about Maud and her reaction to the news about Jamal.

"She said she would talk to the police if they called her, but she really didn't want to even think about Jamal. She said she's been grieving her daughter's death for thirty-five years now, and the pain is more like a distant ache and not the raw pain she had felt for years. She said she was afraid talking to the police about it would open the wound."

"I can understand that," Sophie responded, knowing too well the effort it took to keep that kind of pain at bay. Her husband had been gone for ten years now, and yet any mention of the nursing home or Alzheimer's instantly brought the pain to the forefront of her mind. "But she agreed to talk with them?"

"She did, and Charles called the New Orleans police department and was able to speak with the investigating officer."

"Was he interested?" Sophie asked.

"He was, in fact. He told Charles he had his own suspicions about the guy, but there was no tangible evidence. So at least they'll look more closely now."

As they pulled up in front of Running Stitches, Sarah saw that there were no parking spaces near the shop. "You get out here, Sophie, and I'll park up the street." Sophie started to object but decided to take her friend up on the offer.

"I'll take both of our tote bags in," Sophie announced as she climbed out of the car.

When Sarah walked into the shop a few minutes later, she was pleased to see that all the members of the club had come and were excitedly chatting.

Ruth had set up an extra worktable to accommodate everyone comfortably.

Sophie had saved Sarah a seat at the table with Caitlyn, Frank, and the two sisters who did their quilting. Christina told Sarah that the sports quilt they were quilting for her was almost complete, and they arranged a time for Sarah to pick it up.

"I'm delighted to see so many people here tonight," Delores began, and the room became quiet. "What I'm going to be showing you is the traditional English paper-piecing technique as it was practiced in England back in the 1700s and later in this country in the early 1800s. What we'll actually be doing will be a bit simpler since we don't have to use scraps of newspaper or old wallpaper like they did back then," she added with a chuckle.

Delores had prepared kits that the students purchased from Ruth ahead of time. They included pieces of fabric in various colors, hexagon-shaped papers, and a book on English paper piecing. "What we'll be doing is placing a paper template on your fabric and cutting the fabric a quarter of an inch larger all the way around."

"I thought there was a plastic template for cutting out the fabric that included the seam allowance," Christina said.

"Not in the 1700s," Delores chuckled. "But we have them now, and you can get them from Ruth if you decide to continue with paper piecing. For now, we're going to do it the way it was originally done by the early settlers."

"We're going to be making this small table topper. We'll start by making seven hexagons and connecting them to form a flower, or *rosette*, as they're called." Delores held up a rosette she had made prior to the class and pointed out the seven hexagons, saying, "One in the middle and six round it. Then we'll make a few more rosettes and connect them to other rosettes, forming what is called a mosaic design." She then held up a completed table topper for the group to see the finished product.

The group asked questions about color selection, and Delores directed them to the first few pages in their book.

"What about all these other shapes in the book?" Allison asked.

"We'll be using hexagons for our project, but you can use the English paper-piecing technique when working with many different shapes: apple cores, clamshells, diamonds, octagons, circles, squares, even triangles. The technique is generally the same."

Once everyone had at least one piece of their fabric cut out, Delores continued, demonstrating as she talked. "I like to fold one seam allowance down over the paper and catch it with a pin or a paper clip. At this point, we have two choices. If our papers were thinner, we'd be basting the seam allowances to the paper with long stitches."

"All the way through the paper?"

"Yes, but the stitches and the papers would be removed later. That was the very earliest method of English paper piecing. Later they began to simply turn the seam allowance over the paper and take a stitch in each corner to hold them in place."

Delores explained the process as she demonstrated it. "Quilters began doing it this way as well in the early nineteenth century. We'll use this technique since our papers are made of a light cardboard and it would be tough to sew through them."

"I have a friend who uses a temporary fabric glue stick to attach the seam allowance to the paper," one of the women commented. "It's much easier."

"Yes. Once we've done a few this way, I'll talk about some of the modern innovations that make this process much easier, such as using glue sticks or even iron-on adhesive papers that dissolve when you wash the quilt. We'll also talk about a modern version of English paper piecing that's becoming very popular among experienced quilters, in which hexagons of various sizes are pieced and then arranged to form intricate designs. We'll talk about that next week, but tonight we'll be concentrating on the traditional method."

Frank, who wasn't confident about his hand stitching, asked whether the hexagons could be made by machine, and Delores told him that it's certainly possible, but that she prefers doing them by hand. "I enjoy having a portable project that I can carry with me," Delores added, "and I find it very relaxing."

Delores continued. "We'll be making nine rosettes and connecting them to make our table topper, but as you can see in your book, there are numerous looks you can achieve with rows of hexagons. If you look again at the quilt on the cover, the Grandmother's Flower Garden, you'll see that the pattern is simply hexagons similar to the ones you're making. The choice of color placement creates the design. The larger rosettes on the cover have another row of hexagons—one yellow hexagon in the center, six mauve ones around that, and twelve multicolored ones on the outside row."

"What about those white ones?" Frank asked.

"In a Grandmother's Flower Garden, a row of white hexagons is placed between each rosette to form what is called the *garden path*."

"I'd like to make that quilt," Sophie whispered to Sarah. "It would make a wonderful wedding present," she added wistfully. Sarah raised her eyebrows and nodded her agreement.

"How do you connect the hexagons?" Caitlyn asked, holding up the two she had completed. Delores then demonstrated the tiny whipstitching method used to sew them together.

With Delores' guidance, the class continued cutting and stitching their hexagons while she walked around, offering individual help as needed. Sophie, with her experience in hand piecing, had completed an entire rosette and held it up for everyone to see. "This is fun," she declared.

Every participant had several completed rosettes in front of them by the end of the class. "Keep working on these at home, and when we meet next week, we'll talk about any problems you're having."

Later, as they were driving home, Sarah wondered aloud if she could possibly reproduce the *Memories* quilt using its layout and similar colors as a guide. "Just in case I have to give it up one day," she added.

"Why would you have to give it up?" Sophie asked, looking surprised.

"I might find someone it should belong to."

"You don't think it should belong to you?" Sophie asked.

"In my heart, I think it does," she responded pensively. "But I don't know if I'll be keeping it. I feel compelled to find out where it came from, and I don't know where that might lead."

Chapter 12

A few days later, Charles went into Sarah's sewing room where she sat with a pile of fabric hexagons in front of her. "What are all those for?" he asked, picking up one to examine it.

"I'm putting them together in sets," she responded, reaching for one of her completed flowers. The hexagons had been connected with the whipstitches Delores had demonstrated, and Sophie had helped her perfect them. Sarah pointed out how she had placed one in the middle and six of a different color around it. "Then I chose a third color and added a ring of twelve to complete the flower."

"And where did all that fabric come from?" he asked, looking at the piles of fabric scraps stacked by color on the worktable.

"I raided the scrap boxes in Ruth's back room. I was looking for fabrics that remind me of the colors and designs in the *Memories* quilt."

"Are you planning to make one just like the one you already have?" he asked, trying to understand.

"I'm going to copy it as close as I can. I want to have one in case I lose this one to someone with a more legitimate claim to it."

"How could there be a more legitimate claim?" Charles asked, looking confused. "You bought it fair and square."

"True, but if I find someone from the family of the woman who made it, I would feel obligated to return it to them. The quilt is depending on me to ..." but she stopped talking suddenly, not wanting to finish her sentence. She realized that what she was about to say would sound bizarre to her husband, and she didn't want to try to explain. She wasn't even sure she *could* explain. She just knew she felt a strong responsibility to discover what she could about the quilt.

"Anyway," she continued, "figuring out how it's made is helping me get to know the quilt better."

Charles remained silent, trying to absorb what Sarah had said. She was beginning to sound a bit mystical, and that just didn't seem like his wife, but he decided not to question her.

"So," he said changing the subject, "I came in to tell you that I've had luck tracking down the Andersons."

"Really?" Sarah responded, laying her sewing down and looking up at her husband who had moved over to sit on the futon where he had tossed his notebook earlier.

"The boys had apparently moved away some time ago. I haven't located either one of them yet, but their parents, Susan and Philip Anderson, remained here in Middletown. I found a death certificate for Phillip dated thirteen years ago, but the wife is apparently still living in their original neighborhood."

"Where their house burned down?"

"Well, where the house they were renting burned down, but it seems they were able to buy a house just up the street from there."

"I'm not sure I'd want to do that myself …"

"Well, they had school-age kids and probably friends in the neighborhood. Remember, they lived in that rental at least fifteen years. Maybe they just didn't want to resettle."

"Good point," Sarah responded. "When can we talk to Mrs. Anderson?"

"I was wondering, since she's in her seventies and apparently alone now, perhaps you'd like to speak to her by yourself or maybe with Sophie? She just might be more comfortable."

"I agree. I'll give Mrs. Anderson a call in the morning, but I think I'll go alone." Her friend Sophie had become deeply engrossed in her hexagons, having decided to follow the directions in the book and make the actual Grandmother's Flower Garden quilt as a wedding present for Martha and Timothy.

Sarah had originally intended to make them a quilt herself, but she didn't want to steal Sophie's thunder. She and Charles were talking about offering to pay for the honeymoon Martha and Tim had been talking about. They both loved water sports and were looking at nearby resorts, but Charles had suggested flying them to a more exotic place—"a honeymoon they'll never forget," he had said. *Not that anyone is likely to forget their honeymoon, no matter where it is*, Sarah thought.

* * * * *

"Excuse the mess," Mrs. Anderson said as she led Sarah into the living room crowded with boxes, some sealed and others partially packed. There were stacks of plates and cooking utensils on a card table in the center of the room, along with wrapping paper and rolls of tape. "I'm moving out to Oregon to live with my daughter. No one left here," she added. "It's bad when you outlive your friends and family. Lost one son in the Gulf War, one to cancer, and now just Alice is left. She's retiring this year and wants me to come live with her."

"It's good you can be together." Sarah figured Mrs. Anderson was at least seventy. "Do you have anyone to help you with all this?" Sarah asked, looking at the boxes and piles waiting to be packed.

"I've hired movers, but I wanted to do my own packing. There's lots of stuff to get rid of, and I'm the only one who can make those decisions."

Mrs. Anderson offered Sarah coffee, but Sarah declined, saying, "I don't want to take up much of your time. I know you're very busy."

"So what's this about the quilt?" the woman asked. "You said you had some questions about that old quilt I lost in the fire."

Sarah told her about buying the quilt from a thrift shop and that she was trying to find out something about its history. She had brought a photograph, not wanting to handle the quilt any more than necessary. She pulled it out of her purse and showed it to Mrs. Anderson.

The woman laughed and responded almost sarcastically, "It sure hasn't improved with age. How did you folks find out that it had belonged to me? That was thirty-some years ago."

"It's a long story, but briefly, I was able to find the woman who had it most of those years."

"And how did she get her hands on it?" Mrs. Anderson asked suspiciously. "I thought it burned up."

"Her grandson gave it to her. She didn't know it then, but unfortunately, he and his brother had stolen it the night that your house burned."

"We lost everything that night, what with the fire and then the looting," Mrs. Anderson responded angrily. "Those boys should have been punished."

"Well, Mrs. Anderson, they aren't boys anymore. They're in their forties, and they *are* being punished—not for that, of course, but they're both in prison."

"Good," the woman sputtered.

"The younger boy, Darnell, is in jail in Texas on drug charges, and he's the one that indirectly led me to you. Jerome, his brother, is in prison probably for the rest of his life over in Hamilton. They are ..."

"Wait. Are you talking about Jerome and Darnell Davis?"

"You knew them?" Sarah responded with surprise.

"Everyone in the neighbor knew them. Three boys. The two younger ones, Jerome and Darnell, were nothing but trouble. They lived just up the block back then. Mrs. Davis, their mother, died back in the 80s I think. The father took two of the boys to live with their grandmother—at least that's what people said. Anyway, the father stayed in the house with the older boy for a few months until he ran off."

"The boy ran off?" Sarah gasped.

"No, they both just vanished one day. The house sat there empty for nearly two years before anyone did anything. It was a terrible eyesore until someone finally called the city."

"What did they do?"

"I don't know for sure. The city came out, and the next thing we knew the house was up for sale, foreclosure I think it was. Never saw any of them again. So you say those are the boys that stole our stuff, Jerome and Darnell?"

"Yes. I'm sorry to say they are the ones, and the only thing that was retrieved, as far as I know, was your quilt." Again, Sarah felt the sadness of knowing she was going to have to part with the quilt. This woman was the rightful owner. "I can bring it to you tomorrow if you'd like ..."

"That old thing?" Sue Anderson responded, brushing the idea away with her hand. "Keep it. I never wanted it in the first place. I just stuck it in the back of our linen closet and never used it. My sister Marilee gave that old thing to us as a wedding present. Can you imagine that? My own sister, and that's the best she could do. My Phil and I bought her a beautiful set of china when she married that fool, and that's the best she could do for us. No, I never want to see that thing."

Sarah's heart leaped with joy when she realized the quilt was still hers to keep—at least for now. "How long ago did she give it to you, Mrs. Anderson?"

"We would have been married fifty years come September. It was back in the summer of 1966 that she gave it to us." Sarah saw a look of melancholy briefly cross the woman's face. "Phil's been gone now thirteen years."

"Sorry," Sarah responded compassionately.

As Sarah was preparing to leave, she thanked Mrs. Anderson and wished her well with her upcoming move when she suddenly turned back and said. "Oh, by the way, do you know where your sister got the quilt?"

"Some junk shop I suppose. She always hung out in those places. She tried to tell me it was a valuable antique. Now, what would I want with a valuable antique anyway?"

"Would you mind if I talked to your sister? I'd like to ask her exactly how she got it."

"Can't do that; Marilee died last year. Liver cancer. I can give you the old fool's number if you want to talk to him, but he probably won't know anything about it." She jotted down the name, Harry Wilkinson, and his phone number. "Don't tell him I sent you. He says I'm an old busybody, but then I say he's an old fool, so I guess we're about even," she chuckled as she held the screen door open for Sarah.

Sarah was surprised when Susan suddenly reached out and gave her a gentle pat on the shoulder. "Give that old quilt a good home," she said. "I felt bad after it was gone that I'd kept it up in that closet all those years. It deserved better." She turned abruptly and closed the door.

* * * * *

"Interesting," Charles said.

"Yes," Sarah responded excitedly. "We have one more piece of the quilt's story."

"Well, that's interesting, too, but I meant about the guy running off so abruptly."

"The guy?"

"Jamal Davis."

"Charles!"

"Well, why would he do that? Was he running from the police?" Charles asked rhetorically.

"Were they looking for him?" she responded in a disinterested tone.

"Not that I know of, but maybe he was aware that they should be …"

"Charles, you promised. Leave it alone."

"But he may have done it again."

"We don't know that he *ever* did it—assuming you're suggesting he killed his wives."

"And you think we should just let him get away with it?"

"I think," Sarah said, her voice having raised an octave, "that you should do exactly what you've done. You notified the New Orleans investigator about the possibility, and you've put them in touch with Maud. Let them do their job. And please try to remember that you're retired. You know what the doctor said about stress, and this Jamal thing has the potential of bringing on more stress than you should be trying to handle."

"Nonsense," her husband remarked as he walked out of the room. "Total nonsense. No doctor knows what I can handle," she heard him mumble as he walked down the hall toward his computer room.

Sarah sighed deeply. She really didn't want to be nagging her husband, but the thought of losing him terrified her. *I can't go through that again*, she told herself.

Chapter 13

"And why am I even considering this in the first place?" Martha continued with the rant she had started the moment Sarah picked up the phone. "I've been perfectly happy as a single woman. Why would I give all that up to listen to a middle-aged man trying to find himself?"

"What do you mean?" Sarah asked cautiously.

"He hates the idea of sitting home while I go off to work. He says it's a man's place to work."

"Does he want you to quit?"

Martha was quiet for a moment. "He never said that, but I don't think so. He just seems to think he should be working, too."

"What's happened with the coaching he does at the Center and the classes he's been taking?"

"He's still doing all that. He just seems to think he should be going off to a job that provides a paycheck. I remind him that he did that for nearly forty years and that he's retired and receiving an excellent retirement check, but just the fact that I'm the only one working seems to threaten his manhood. What's wrong with men, anyway?" she asked but didn't wait for an answer before continuing her rant. "It's ridiculous, and I'm getting sick of it. Did you know that he's been in contact with the companies that are waiting for something to happen with this Keystone pipeline controversy? He has this fantasy that he'll become involved if it's ever approved."

"I wouldn't worry about that, Martha. That would be years from now, if ever."

"I know. I just wish he could relax and enjoy the life we've talked about having. I'm really beginning to wonder if this is a mistake ..."

"I hate to say it, Martha, but I can see his point. He's pretty young to be a retiree. Has he looked for work?"

"You know he has," Martha snapped. "Don't you remember last fall when all he could find was that job in Pennsylvania, and he almost left us all to take it? There's nothing here in town for a man his age, especially with the economy being what it is," she added angrily.

Don't take it out on me, Sarah thought and wanted to say but didn't. "Do you want to come over and talk?" Sarah asked her daughter.

"No. There's nothing left to say. I'm going to have to figure this out for myself, but in the meantime, leave the tags on that dress. I may not be needing it," she added and hung up the phone.

Sarah sighed and sat down at the kitchen table in front of a cup of coffee that had grown cold. She didn't know what to tell her daughter; she just knew that her daughter's relationship with Timothy was the best thing that had ever happened to her, not to mention the bond she had with Timothy's daughter. Penny was accepting Martha in the role of mother, and Sarah couldn't stand the thought of Penny losing that again. *What can I do to keep this from happening?* she wondered, but no immediate answer came to mind.

She was still sitting there when Charles walked in the door. She'd been eager to discuss it with him.

"Charles," she began.

"Wait," he countered. "I've got something fascinating to tell you. I spent a couple of hours with Susan Anderson's brother-in-law."

"Who?" Sarah asked, her mind having left the issue of the quilt and the Andersons.

"You remember. The guy Mrs. Anderson referred to as 'the old fool.' Her sister's husband."

"Of course. Did he know anything about the quilt?"

"He sure did."

Sarah tried hard to put her mind on the project she and her husband had been working on and set her concerns about Martha aside for the time being. "Tell me about it," she said as she dumped her cold coffee out and poured them each a fresh cup. She reached for the low-fat oatmeal cookies she had made earlier but noticed that her husband wrinkled up his nose and frowned. She pushed the cookie jar aside and sat down. "What did he say?"

"He remembers the very day she brought it home."

"And?" she responded without much interest.

"He said we can come over tomorrow and talk about it in person. Actually, he sounded lonely and just wanted some company."

When Sarah didn't respond, Charles was astonished that his wife seemed to have lost her previous enthusiasm about the quilt. She had been so eager to receive every new piece of information either of them discovered. "What's wrong, hon?" he asked, and Sarah began to sob.

* * * * *

The next day, Sarah and Charles arrived at Harry Wilkinson's house, better known to Sarah as "the old fool"; however, she was surprised when he opened the door with a broad smile and a friendly greeting. "Come on in, folks. What can I get you? I just made a pitcher of sweet tea."

"Sounds great," Charles responded before Sarah could object to the sugar. She decided to let it go.

"Yes. Thank you, Mr. Wilkinson," she responded.

"Call me Harry," he replied, followed by the long overused comeback, "Mr. Wilkinson was my father." They all chuckled appropriately and followed him into the living room. "Have a seat. I'll be right back."

He returned moments later with three large tumblers and an antique glass pitcher filled with tea. "I float a few sprigs of mint in my tea. Hope you folks don't mind."

"I love it that way," Sarah responded. She always included one bag of mint tea along with the regular tea bags when she made iced tea herself.

Once they were seated and had gone through the ritualistic small talk about the weather, Sarah could see the conversation was moving on to politics. She immediately interrupted, knowing politics was likely to take over the entire visit once she realized that the men were on opposite ends of the spectrum.

"My husband told me that you remember the quilt that you and your wife gave your sister-in-law back in 1966," she said.

"There's no way I could ever forget that old quilt," he responded as he sat back in his chair and put his feet up, apparently prepared for a lengthy visit. "Marilee and I had our worst fight over that thing. I told her it wasn't appropriate as a wedding gift. It looked like it was a hundred years old and all worn out. I knew her sister would hate it, and she did."

"She did?" Sarah asked, surprised that Susan would have told her sister how she felt about it.

"She didn't exactly say so. It's just that over the next years, we never saw it in her house. If she even kept it, I suppose it burned up in the fire. Why are you folks asking about it anyway?"

Sarah told him the story of how she came by it and briefly explained where it had been in the meantime. She neglected to suggest that it might be a valuable piece of history. "So," she added, "I'm interested in finding out something about its history, and I was hoping you would know how your wife happened to have it."

"I surely do, and that's partly why I didn't want her to give it as a gift. She didn't pay a penny for it. A good friend of hers, Agatha Tarkington, gave it to her."

Excitedly, Sarah asked if he knew how to reach Agatha.

"Sorry, but she died long ago from cancer, sometime in the 1960s. Anyway, someone had passed that old quilt to Agatha's mother back in the 1800s, and Agatha told us it was some kind of family treasure. Agatha got it after her mother died, but she really didn't seem to care anything about it. She just said her mother had wanted it to stay in the family, but Agatha never married and never had kids. There was no family to take it."

"Didn't Agatha have aunts and uncles? There must have been someone in the family to give it to."

"According to Marilee, Agatha had no family at all."

"So Agatha gave the quilt to your wife?" Sarah asked, surprised that the woman would give away something that had been passed down in her family.

"My Marilee was always interested in antiques, and Agatha was a good friend. Agatha knew her days were numbered—she thought my wife would like to have it since she was into antiques and all. Like I said, there was no family to pass it on to."

"But your wife didn't keep it. She gave it away?"

"Yep, she sure did. Marilee never really wanted it, but she kept it out of respect for Agatha. After Agatha died, Marilee decided to give it to her sister Susan as a wedding present, and, like I said, that was the worst fight we ever had. I wanted to buy something nice for Susan and Phil, but Marilee had her mind made up."

Once the questions about the quilt were exhausted, the men returned to politics, but Sarah intervened, suggesting that they needed to get home. "We left the dog in the yard, and I'm afraid he'll start barking and disturb the neighbors." Charles looked at his wife and knew she was simply ready to leave. She wasn't making up the part about Barney being outside, but the pool had been freshly filled, and they both knew Barney was probably laying on his back in the water and ecstatically happy.

Once they got into the car, Sarah said, "This sounds like a dead end to me."

"Not necessarily," Charles responded. "There could be relatives, great-aunts, or cousins maybe. You never know."

Sarah asked if he thought he could find out anything about Agatha's family tree on the internet.

"Maybe," he responded, "but I might have to join one of those websites where you can track down your ancestors."

"Let's call Paula," Sarah suggested. Paula was a friend that Sarah met in her water aerobics class the previous year. "She was very involved in searching for her own ancestors, and she'll help us get started."

"Good idea," Charles responded, but he seemed distracted.

"You're turning the wrong way," Sarah said, suddenly realizing that Charles wasn't headed toward Cunningham Village.

"I know. I want to make a stop on the way." He pulled up in front of the firehouse and indicated that Sarah should go in with him. Once inside, he introduced his wife to Chief Deegan. "Deeg and I have known each other for over thirty years," Charles said.

"Glad to meet you," Sarah responded, a bit confused about why they were there but gracious all the same.

Charles reached into his pocket and pulled out a folder sheet of paper. "Hope this is okay," he said as he handed the sheet to the fire chief.

"Thanks, Charlie. The county requires three references, and this does it. The pipeline had great things to say. I think we can consider it official. Do you want to tell your wife now?"

"What are you men talking about?" Sarah asked.

"Deeg and I have worked out a solution to Timothy's problem."

"You have?" she said, looking surprised. "What?"

"I'm going to offer him a part-time job right here," Chief Deegan responded. "Charlie here came to me with the idea, and I liked it."

"I didn't know a thing about this," Sarah responded, "but this is just perfect for Tim." *And this will make Martha so happy*, she thought.

"I decided not to mention it," Charles explained, "because I didn't want to get their hopes up until Deeg had a chance to check it out."

"I'm going to call him this week," the chief said. "I was really impressed with the guy when he was here helping old Charlie with that massive search of his. That young man is some worker!"

"He did most of the searching and organizing that day," Charles added.

"And that's exactly what they'll be needing around here."

"Are you planning to retire?" Sarah asked.

"I sure am someday, but not now. What I'm hoping to do is cut my hours back to half-time for the next few years. My wife's been sick for a while now, and I want to spend more time with her." He dropped his eyes, and Sarah could tell he was feeling very emotional, but he quickly continued. "Everyone we've talked to about the job is either unqualified or wants full time, and we only want a part-time guy."

Before leaving, Charles asked if he could show Sarah the Quonset hut where he had located the information on the 1985 fire. They walked behind the station to the annex, and the room filled from floor to ceiling with boxes took her breath away. "What a terrible job that must have been," she exclaimed. "How did you ever do it?"

"I had help," he reminded her.

After thanking the chief and heading to their car, Charles got the hug of appreciation Sarah had been saving for him. "Thank you," she whispered. "Do you think I should call Martha?"

"No. Deeg will be calling Tim. Just let the guys handle it from here." He leaned over and gently kissed her cheek. "And leave my name out of it, okay?"

"Yes, that's best," she replied. "Tell me about Deeg's wife," she asked as they were driving home.

"Parkinson's," he responded. "She's had it since we worked together, but it's progressing more rapidly the past year or two. When I knew her, it was just the tremors, but now Deeg says she's not getting around at all. She's got a caregiver, but that's just not the same."

"I can see why he wants to be home. I'm surprised he's not retiring."

"Deeg won't consider it, and honestly, I think they need the money, what with her medical care."

They drove on in silence, each lost in thought. Sarah wondered about their own future and what was in store for them. *Just enjoy the moment*, she told herself as she reached for her husband's hand. "Thank you for helping Tim," she said.

Still holding her hand, he lifted it to his lips and gently kissed it.

Chapter 14

"Sarah, you have a call."

"Take a message, please. I just started kneading this dough, and I have sticky stuff up to my elbows."

"Can't do that," Charles responded. "This is a critical call. I'll put it on speaker."

Suddenly words rang out across the kitchen. Charles had set the speaker volume on high. "Grandma, I love my sports quilt. It's so cool," the young voice called out. "Man, just wait 'til Buddy sees this. None of my friends have anything this awesome. Thanks, Grandma."

"You're very welcome, Jimmy. I enjoyed making it for you."

"Uh, Grandma?" he said, sounding hesitant and somewhat embarrassed.

"Yes?"

"Could you not call me Jimmy anymore?"

"Okay, but why?"

"It's a little kids' name."

"So what shall I call you?" Sarah asked as she winked at Charles.

"Jim," he responded, "or James if you want. Just not *Jimmy.*"

"Done. From now on, you're my grandson, Jim or James, never *Jimmy.*"

"Thanks," he responded. "And thanks for the quilt. I gotta go. Bye."

"You're very welcome, Jim. Tell your family hello from me."

"I will," he responded with a smile in his voice.

After Charles had hung up the phone, they both burst out laughing. "They're becoming teenagers younger and younger, aren't they?"

"They sure are," Sarah responded. "I almost put a label on that quilt that read, *For my grandson Jimmy.* It's a good thing I ran out of time."

* * * * *

"Detective Lawrence called while you were out. He said he tried your cell phone, but it was off. He wants you to call right away. So who is Detective Lawrence?" Sarah asked after delivering the message to Charles as he walked in the door from the garage. "And why wasn't your cell phone on?" she added.

"Okay. Let me get in the house and pour a glass of lemonade, and I'll answer your questions." Charles was dripping sweat, and Sarah knew he had been working out hard at the gym. She hoped he wasn't overdoing it but decided not to ask, at least not right now. He wasn't making eye contact, however, and she was getting concerned.

"Charles?"

"I said I'll just be a minute." He drank most of the glass of lemonade without stopping and wiped his forehead with his workout towel. He refilled the glass and sat down at the table. "First of all, my phone was in my locker for ten minutes while I was in the sauna, and if he really wanted to talk to me, you'd think he'd have left a message."

"He told me he did," Sarah responded as she placed the turkey sandwich and salad in front of him.

Charles checked his phone and mumbled, "He did. I'll listen to it later."

"He told me it was important," Sarah added.

"Could we just eat lunch in peace?" he snapped. "I'll handle it later."

Shocked by her husband's behavior, she started to storm out of the kitchen but turned to confront him. "Charles, what's going on? I didn't do anything to deserve this attitude."

"Okay," he responded lowering his head and looking deflated. "I'm sorry I snapped at you. It's just that this detective, Bud Lawrence down in Louisiana, wants Maud Templeton to come down and testify before the grand jury. They're looking at Jamal for his wife's murder, and the prosecutor wants to present Maud's story about the untimely death of his first wife."

"And this involves you?"

"Lawrence wants me to see if I can get her there, perhaps even take her there. I don't mind doing it, but I didn't want to tell you yet. I knew it would send you up the wall since I've promised to stay out of this one."

Sarah had to pinch back a smile as she watched him struggle with his confession. Finally, she rolled her eyes and chuckled. "Okay. I get it. So tell me more about what's going on. Maybe you and I could both go and eat some jambalaya."

"I understand New Orleans seafood is phenomenal, fresh right out of the Gulf," he added, trying to encourage what appeared to be her more accepting response to the situation. "We could make it a mini vacation."

"What would we do with Maud while we were mini vacationing?" she asked rhetorically.

"Ah. I didn't think about that."

"But," Sarah said, giving him a playful look, "It still might be fun. We could at least have one good meal while we're there, or we could even get Maud a room and stay over one night."

"I'll call him now," Charles responded with a sigh of relief. Sarah knew he was torn between his love of crime solving and his love for her. He didn't seem to get it, though, that her concern was his health and well-being. Her last talk with his doctor had scared her.

"Let me know when to start packing," she called as he left the room with his cell phone already on his ear.

They slept late the next morning, having talked into the night about the case against Jamal, about Maud, and about the trip. They decided to both go the next morning to talk with Maud and, if she was willing, they'd accompany her to New Orleans the following Monday. Detective Lawrence had told them the hearing was scheduled for Tuesday, and he had assured them there were funds available for airline tickets and hotel rooms for both Maud and Charles. "But if she doesn't want to go," Sarah had said, "we drop it. I don't want to force her into anything. The woman's been through enough because of that man."

"I agree," Charles had said as he turned out the light and reached for her hand. "Thank you for understanding."

Chapter 15

"And you thought I wouldn't want to go?" Maud Templeton responded incredulously. "If I can do anything to get that man locked up for the rest of his life, I'm in. Who's driving?"

"It's at least a twelve-hour drive," Sarah replied, "and that's too much for any of us. Charles will get our tickets and we'll fly."

"We'll what?" Maud shrieked. "There's no way I'm getting onto an airplane. I've made it eighty-one years without being up in the sky, and I'm not starting now. I'll get Gilbert to drive me."

"Who's Gilbert?" Sarah asked.

"He's my grandson," the voice behind them said. Bertha was standing in the hall just outside of Maud's bedroom. "I've been listening to what you people are trying to do here. I think it would be very hard for Maud to travel all the way down there, and it's probably going to be a waste of time anyway. They aren't trying him for Clarissa's murder, right?"

"Correct," Charles said. "They're looking at him for the possible murder of his second wife. The prosecution thinks it will help their case for Maud to tell them about her suspicions."

"Maud, I think you and I should talk about this without these folks."

"The hearing is next Tuesday, Mrs. Washington. We'll have to make plans right away …"

"I know. You get on out of here and come back in a couple of hours. I just need some time alone with Maud."

As they pulled away from the curb, Sarah turned to Charles and said, "What do you think? Is Bertha going to talk Maud out of going?"

"I think so. She's made it her mission to take care of her friend. Remember, she tracked her down in that shelter and gave her a home."

"What should we do?" she asked.

"I think we should do exactly what you suggested last night. We told her about the prosecutor's request, and we offered to go with her. And now the decision is hers."

"Yes, but it was very clear to me that she wanted to do this. You saw her initial reaction. I'm afraid Bertha is going to talk her out of it."

"For once," her husband responded, "I'm going to be the one who says that we let them work it out themselves. Let's get some lunch. We were in such a hurry this morning we skimped on breakfast, and I'm hungry."

"They serve brunch until 11:00 at the Village Diner. Let's go there."

"You got it," he said as he made a U-turn and headed for the diner. It was one of his favorite places back when he was with the department. They were open all night, and he often stopped for sausage and eggs with a side of fries smothered in country gravy on his way home when he'd been working nights. *I guess that's not what I'll be ordering today*, he told himself reluctantly.

As he was paying the bill an hour or so later, his cell phone rang, and Sarah glanced at the display as he picked it up. He had left his number with Maud and said to call when she wanted them to return. "It's Maud," she said.

Charles' side of the conversation didn't reveal much. He said "Okay" three times and ended with, "We'll see you then."

"So?" Sarah said as they were walking toward the car.

"Maud wants to talk to us."

"Did she say what she decided?"

"Nope. Just told me she wanted to talk to us."

They were both silent as they drove back to Bertha's house. They had talked about it over breakfast and were both comfortable with whatever Maud decided. "We'll be able to tell the prosecutor that we tried," Charles had said.

Bertha Washington opened the door before they had a chance to knock and ushered them into the kitchen, where Maud was sitting at the table drinking coffee. "Have a seat, folks," Bertha said. "Coffee?"

"We just had coffee," Sarah said, "but thank you."

"Actually, I'll take one if you don't mind," Charles said as he sat.

Once they were settled, Bertha excused herself, saying, "You folks have lots to talk about. I'll be upstairs if you need me."

"Well," Maud began. "Bertha is dead set against me going all that way in the car. You said it was twelve hours, but

Bertha said what with me having to stop every few hours it'd be much longer than that."

"Maud," Sarah began. "Remember when we told you about this, we said it's completely up to you. We understand if you don't want to do it."

"Didn't say I don't want to do it." Turning to Charles, she said, "You told me that this would help to get that monster locked up, and I want that. I want that for my Clarissa. I know I said that I'd never fly, but if you really think it will help put him away, I'll grit my teeth—what few I have—and get on that plane. Will you sit with me?" she asked, turning to Sarah.

"Most planes have three seats in a row, and you can sit in the middle between us," Sarah responded as she reached across the table and patted Maud's shaky hand. "We'll be with you every minute."

"One more thing," Maud said. "Do you think I could spend a few hours with my cousin? You said New Orleans, right?"

"Yes. Is that where your cousin lives?"

Maud smiled. "It sure is. I haven't seen Bessie for over fifty years. She's in her nineties, and this might be our last chance. I called her this morning, and she was really excited about me coming. Her grandson can drive her to the courthouse to be with me, and she said they could take me back to her house, but I told her you folks would be coming right back home."

"This works out just perfectly, Maud. Charles and I wanted to spend a couple of days down there, too. Will it be okay with your cousin for you to stay with her for two or three days?"

"I'm sure it will. This is turning out to be an adventure," Maud said excitedly. "Who would've thought it?"

Maud used Charles' cell phone to call her cousin and make the arrangements. Before they left, he called Detective Lawrence to let him know they were coming and to verify the time and place for the hearing.

"I'll make our airline reservations when we get home, and Sarah will call to let you know exactly when we'll be picking you up."

"What should I bring?"

"Just a small bag, Maud," Sarah responded, "so we can take it on the plane with us. You'll only be there a couple of days. If you have any questions, call me." Sarah wrote down the number for her own cell phone and handed it to Maud.

"You and your husband have different phone numbers?" she said, looking confused.

Sarah laughed. "Life is getting more complicated every day, Maud. We have a phone at home, and we each have our own cell phones—three phone numbers, a house address, several email addresses …"

"Lordy be," Maud muttered as she got up and rinsed out her cup.

Sarah noticed she wasn't shaking anymore and had a twinkle in her eye as she walked them to the door. "We're gonna get this guy, aren't we?" Maud asked as they were leaving.

"We're going to do our best," Charles replied with a wink.

Maud smiled and watched until they pulled away from the curb.

"She's finally able to do something for her Clarissa," Sarah said hopefully.

* * * * *

While Charles was making their reservations, Sarah put a call into Ruth at the fabric shop. "Ruth, are you busy?"

"I'm totally bored. I haven't had a customer all afternoon, and I'm glad you called. In fact, I was just getting ready to call you and get the phone tree started."

"What's up?"

"I just had a call from Delores. She fell at her daughter's house, and her arm is in a sling. She called to see if we could postpone the class for a week. I was going to ask you if you thought we should just cancel the meeting altogether since Delores' class was all we had planned."

"That's easy for me to answer. I was calling to tell you I can't be there, and I must admit that I'm delighted that I won't be missing Delores' class, but of course I'm sorry she is hurt," she quickly added, realizing her response had sounded very self-serving. "It's just that Charles and I are making an unplanned trip to New Orleans next week."

"Does this have anything to do with the *Memories* quilt?" Ruth asked hopefully.

"Indirectly, yes." Sarah caught her friend up on the progress they had made and told her about tracking down what she hoped would turn out to be the family whose ancestors had made the quilt.

"What's the family name? I might know them."

"The name we have is Tarkington. Agatha Tarkington, but she died in 1976, so you probably wouldn't have known her."

"No, but there's a Tarkington Wing in City Hospital. They might know something about her. I don't know if it's named for her or maybe someone in her family."

Sarah felt a surge of excitement. "This might be the lead we need. Thank you, Ruth. I'll go talk with them tomorrow."

"I know how busy you are," Ruth said. "I'll call your three people and let them know about Tuesday so we can get the word out on the phone tree. Shall I mention that you'll be out of town, as well?"

"Sure, that's fine. You don't need to call Sophie. I'll be seeing her this afternoon, and I'll let her know. For that matter, I'll be telling Caitlyn, too, because I need to call her for pet sitting."

"So that just leaves Frank?"

"Right. I just have the three on my list. Frank will call his friend Sasha. He told me that he only wanted to call one person so he'd be sure to do it right."

"He's an incredible young man," Ruth responded.

"He sure is. He's comfortable with who he is and knows his limitations, yet he's always eager to give something new a try. He's an inspiration to us all."

"So," Ruth said, concluding the conversation rather abruptly when the doorbell jiggled in the background, "Good luck with your Louisiana project, and take some time for fun while you're there."

"We intend to," Sarah responded.

As Sarah hung up, she grabbed a glass of iced tea and sat back down to call Sophie. "Sophie, I have so much to tell you. Can you come over and help me make a list of what to take to New Orleans?" Sarah was grinning as she said it.

"New Orleans? You're going to New Orleans? Why? No, don't answer that—I'll be right over."

Chapter 16

When they picked up Maud on Monday morning, they found her to be somewhere between excited and terrified. They again reassured her about the flight and the hearing. "If God had meant for me to fly …" she began but didn't finish.

"We'll be just fine. It's just like riding a bus," Charles assured her.

"A bus up in the clouds?" she responded sarcastically. "I don't think so."

But once they got seated on the plane, Maud began to settle down. As the aircraft took off, they each held one of her hands, and once they were in the air, she announced reluctantly, "Well, that wasn't so bad."

"Would you like to take a look out the window?" Sarah offered, having taken the window seat so Maud could feel even more protected with Charles on her other side.

"Absolutely not," she announced emphatically. "You might get me up here, but you sure won't get me to look down!"

When the flight attendant came by offering beverages, Maud ordered a cup of tea and was amazed when Sarah pulled out the tray for her. When the attendant returned with Maud's tea and a packet of cookies, she smiled, and Sarah could see her beginning to relax.

"This isn't so bad," Maud muttered aloud to herself. "Not so bad at all."

Maud drank her tea, and the three sat quietly for a while. Suddenly Maud spoke up, saying, "I sure hope I don't see that hateful man."

"Jamal?" Charles asked.

"Of course Jamal. I don't know if I can control my temper around him."

"You won't see him. He's not a part of this hearing," Charles assured her.

"So how are they going to put him in prison if he isn't even there?"

"It isn't actually a trial, Maud. The grand jury just meets with the prosecutor and his witnesses, and they hear all the evidence. Then they decide if there's enough evidence for the case to go to trial."

"So why am I here?" Maud demanded. "I already know he should go to prison."

"You are here so that you can tell the grand jury about your daughter. It will help the prosecutor prove what kind of man he is."

"Hmm. Well as long as he ends up in prison, I don't much care how it happens. He shouldn't be out there enjoying life with my girl in her grave."

Sarah felt a shiver down her spine as she thought what it must be like to have that thought about one's own child. She reached over and patted Maud's hand, which was no longer trembling as it had been when they led her onto the plane.

Wanting to change the subject, she asked Maud about her relationship with Bertha. "You two have been friends for a long time, haven't you?"

"You bet we have. We went to grade school together seventy-some years ago. We were living out in the country about ten miles outside of Middletown. Papa had a dairy farm, but he never did very well. When I was twelve, we moved on over to Hamilton, and he worked in the glass factory until he retired."

"That's still there, isn't it?" Sarah asked. "I think they have tours."

"I heard it was. Ma and I moved back to Middletown after he died, and I met Harold and married him. Our only child, Clarissa, was born in 1955 and died in 1984. She had a short life, poor baby, and not a very good life after she met that man."

"Tell me more about you and Bertha. You got together again after you moved back here?"

"Oh, we kept in touch. She even came to visit us in Hamilton a couple of times. Her folks were pretty well off. Anyway, we stayed friends over the years. I guess I told you that she came to live with me after her husband died. She was pretty broken up and ended up staying on with Clarissa and me for a few years."

"It's very special to have a lifelong friend," Sarah said.

"Oh, we had our ups and downs, that's for sure. Mostly over Clarissa. Bertha never understood the girl like I did. She believed all those lies about drugs and stuff, but she was right there for me when my girl was buried and then again when I had to live in that homeless place."

"What was that like?" Sarah asked.

"Horrible! The worst was having to be outside all day. They push you out early in the morning, and you couldn't come back until evening. Then you had to stand in line to get into the place at night and stand in line again for a shower. I was nearly eighty years old, but that didn't get me any special treatment. Lots of the men were that old."

"How did you get your meals?"

"They served breakfast up the street at the soup kitchen and gave you a bag lunch for later. I usually saved mine for dinner so I could get in line early at the shelter."

"What did you do during the day?" Sarah asked, trying to imagine the life Maud was living.

"I usually walked over to the park so I could sit."

"But then Bertha came for you?"

"Oh, you can't imagine how happy I was to look up one morning and see Bertha talking to the manager. I saw him point at me, and she rushed over, looking more determined than I had ever seen her look. We hugged and suddenly she said, 'Get your stuff, and let's get out of this place.' Been with her ever since."

About that time, the plane hit some turbulence, and Maud grabbed Sarah with one hand and Charles with the other. "It's okay," Charles assured her. "Just a little bump."

"A bump in the sky?" Maud exclaimed. "Skies aren't supposed to be bumpy."

Charles explained about the wind and talked about aerodynamics until Maud's eyes glazed over. "Well, it's stopped now," she said emphatically, implying that he should do the same.

The landing went smoothly, with Maud hanging on to her two protectors until they were safely in the cab and headed toward the hotel where they had booked two rooms for the night.

* * * * *

It was only 9:00 that night when Sarah's cell phone rang. She grabbed it quickly, hoping not to awaken her roommate. Sarah and Charles had decided to ask Maud if she would like for Sarah to stay with her for the night. When they took her to her room earlier, she had looked hesitant to go in, and Sarah realized she was probably worried about being alone. Unfortunately for Sarah, Maud went to bed at 8:00, long before Sarah's usual bedtime.

She whispered her hello but noticed that Maud had opened her eyes. "I'm going to step next door and talk to my daughter," she said to Maud, who nodded her agreement and snuggled down deeper under the covers. She wasn't accustomed to air conditioning and had asked for an extra blanket.

"Sorry, Martha," Sarah whispered into the phone as she slipped down the hall to their room.

"What's going on?"

Sarah caught her daughter up on the happenings since arriving in New Orleans, including why she was whispering. She was now in the room with Charles, where she could speak freely since he was wide awake and reading a detective novel.

"I'm glad things are working out there," Martha was saying. "I was worried about you getting that woman onto the plane. Anyway, I'm calling to give you some incredible news. Tim has a job!"

"Really? Where?" Sarah asked, assuming it was probably with the fire chief. Since they hadn't heard anything since they met with Deegan, she wasn't sure what had happened with that.

"He was offered a part-time job at the firehouse. He met the fire chief the day he went out there to help Charles, and when he called Tim last week, it was quite a shock."

Apparently, Sarah thought, *the fire chief didn't tell Timothy about Charles intervening on his behalf.* She knew Charles would be glad. He had told Sarah that Timothy would feel better thinking he got the job totally on his own.

"I'm so glad, Martha. I know this is a relief to you."

"It is, and with it being only part time, Tim will be able to continue with his classes and with coaching the senior ball team." Timothy had organized and was coaching a softball team at Cunningham Village, which had led to several other senior communities doing the same thing. They now traveled between communities competing and called themselves the Elder League.

"Tell him how excited we are for him … for both of you, actually. Does this mean I can take the tags off the dress?" she teased.

"Mom, I wasn't serious about that."

"I know."

Chapter 17

The bailiff called Maud and held the door open for her to enter the courtroom.

"Aren't you folks coming in with me?" she asked, turning to her friends with a pleading look.

"No," Charles responded. "We aren't allowed to be in the room, but we'll be right here waiting when you come out. Just remember what we talked about. Answer the questions the best you can."

Maud entered the room on the arm of the bailiff, who towered over the small, frail woman. She had reached for his arm when she felt her legs become weak as she entered the room. A crowd of people was sitting in what she assumed to be the jurors' seats since there was a short wall in front of them just like on television. But there were far more than she expected—about twice as many. There was no one in the spectator seats, and she wondered why Sarah and Charles couldn't have come in.

The bailiff led her to a seat facing the jurors, and the prosecutor greeted her and thanked her for coming. She had met him when they arrived at the courthouse earlier that day. He then introduced her to the grand jury and asked her if she knew why she had been invited to testify.

"To tell you about Jamal Davis killing my girl, Clarissa."

"His first wife?"

"Yes."

"Tell us about that, Ms. Templeton. Just take your time," he added gently. "Did you see him kill her?" He already knew that she hadn't witnessed it but wanted to get that issue out of the way from the beginning.

"I didn't see it, but I know it happened as sure as we're all sitting here. She'd come to see me, and she'd be all beaten up. Sometimes she had black eyes, and sometimes she was covered with bruises. Once she was wearing a sling, and I'd always ask her what happened."

"Did she tell you?"

"Not the truth. She'd make excuses for him. She'd say she tripped or she bumped into things. When he broke her jaw, she said she slipped and fell against the washing machine. But I always knew the truth, and I knew my daughter was terrified of that beast."

"Did you ever see him hit her?"

"No, sir. He always acted polite around me. He didn't want me to know what was going on."

"Did your daughter ever tell you he was hurting her?"

"No. Like I said, she protected him. I guess she loved him. I don't know why, but once when I took her to the hospital with a broken arm, the doctors asked her lots of questions. They suspected she'd been beaten, and they asked me, too. But Clarissa looked at me with this pleading look, and I just shook my head. Maybe I could have saved my girl if only …"

she stopped talking, remembering what Charles had said. *Just answer the questions, nothing more.*

"Did you ever talk to the police about your suspicions?"

"I surely did, but only after she was gone," she said, fighting tears. "I told them he had killed her, but they didn't believe me."

"Did they say why they didn't believe you?"

"Oh, Jamal—he was a slick one. He could con anybody, and he sure had those cops conned into believing that my girl was a drug addict. They said she died of an overdose, but I know he gave it to her."

"You know that he gave her the overdose?" the prosecutor asked. She hadn't mentioned this in their interview, and he only hoped she had the right answer. He tried never to ask a question when he didn't already know the answer. He was aware that what she had to say wouldn't convict Davis, but she was doing a good job of letting the jurors know what kind of man he probably was. Her story was the typical story of an abuser. Since she hadn't answered, he repeated his question, "Do you know that he administered the fatal dose of drugs?"

"Do I know he did that? I absolutely know that as well as I know my own name. He killed my girl, and if they say it was an overdose of drugs that killed her, then he gave her the overdose."

"But did you see him do it?" he asked, hopefully.

"Of course not. He's not that stupid. But he did it. I know that." The prosecutor sighed imperceptibly.

Once Maud was excused, she joined her friends in the hallway and sat down with a deep sigh. "Was it hard?" Sarah asked.

"It was hard to go back and think about those days, but it wasn't hard to answer the questions. I couldn't prove Jamal killed my girl, but he's not on trial for that anyway. But I sure let them know what kind of man he is." Charles was glad to know that she had a clear understanding of the hearing and the part she had played. *If the man is convicted, she'll know she helped.*

"Aunt Bessie!" Maud cried suddenly. "Over here." She painfully lifted herself off the hard bench and walked toward a very old woman who was crossing the room on a walker. A man who didn't look much younger held her arm.

"Maud, my dear. It's so good to see you," the woman said in a raspy voice. "Gilbert tried to get me to use my wheelchair, but I wanted to meet you standing on my own two feet," she said proudly. The two women hugged and began chattering while Charles and Gilbert shook hands and helped the two women to the two upholstered chairs on the opposite side of the room.

"We'll let you two women visit while Gilbert and I make some plans."

* * * * *

"What shall we do first?" Charles asked after Gilbert drove off with Bessie and Maud in the back seat, both talking at once.

"I think we should grab a taxi and go back to our room to freshen up. Then I'd like to put on comfortable shoes and walk around the French Quarter. I've wanted to do that for years and never expected to have the chance. Maybe we could watch for an interesting place to have a light lunch."

"Why light?" Charles asked. "Are you intending to keep me on that outrageous diet while we're here?"

"I think with all the seafood and vegetables they feature here, you won't have a problem, but I said 'light' because I was hoping we could go really fancy at dinnertime."

"Sounds excellent," he responded.

A short time later, Charles and Sarah were walking toward the river reading the menus displayed in the many restaurants along the way. Their hotel room overlooked the Mississippi, and they decided they'd surely find restaurants nearby. In fact, they found that almost every other storefront was a restaurant. "Look," Charles called to her as he read the menu on the window of a small neighborhood grill. "They have catfish."

"And I should want catfish?" she responded.

"It's tradition," he replied. "Let's eat here."

From the outside, the restaurant looked very casual, and they were surprised to find it more elegant on the inside. They were led to a table on the second floor and offered a seat at the window overlooking the Mississippi. Intending to have a light lunch, they ordered the crawfish dip as an appetizer and decided to split the lunch special. Charles added a carafe of white wine.

When their meal arrived, a seafood stew, Sarah sighed with pleasure. "This is beautiful," she exclaimed, and the waitress smiled.

"I love serving it," she responded. "Folks are always surprised at the variety of things in our stew."

"I didn't read the details on the menu. What's in it besides the shrimp and oysters?"

"It has shrimp, oysters, mussels, pieces of halibut, and crawfish tails. Then for vegetables, it has potatoes, green and red peppers, onions, tomatoes, and of course, mirlitons."

"Mirlitons?" Charles asked.

"Sure. It's the unofficial squash of New Orleans, but I think it's actually a gourd. It's a Louisiana favorite. We even have a festival in the fall celebrating it—the Bywater Mirliton Festival. We grow them in our backyards, and we fry them, stuff them with shrimp, and even pickle them. Like I said, it's a favorite down here. I hope you like it."

As she talked, she was scooping out an even amount of everything to a second bowl since the couple had said they wanted to split the stew. Once she finished, she excused herself to get their bread. Suddenly Sarah remembered and exclaimed, "You didn't get your catfish."

"I'm saving that for dinner."

After lunch, they picked up a walking tour guide for the French Quarter. They visited some of the sites listed and just admired the architecture of others. They went inside the 1850 House, which depicted middle-class life during the period, including furniture, art, and domestic items. "I assume the residents were rather prosperous," Sarah whispered to Charles. A staff member heard her and said that 1850 was a prosperous period in New Orleans, particularly in the French Quarter.

Once they reached the French Market, they were ready to rest, so they found a place to sit and enjoy the music while watching local shoppers and out-of-town visitors peruse the open market. On their way out, Sarah spotted a vendor selling bracelets, and she told Charles she'd like to have one as a remembrance. After looking through the items, she held up a silver chain with a charm in the shape of a shrimp and announced, "This is it." Charles chuckled as he pulled out his credit card.

"Tomorrow I'd like to do this," Charles said, pointing to a poster near the river. Sarah moved closer and read that the Steamboat Natchez, a classic Mississippi riverboat, featured New Orleans jazz and dinner on their evening cruises. "What do you think?" he asked after she had a chance to read it.

"It sounds like the perfect way to end our short getaway. Let's make reservations for tomorrow night."

Exhausted by the end of the day, they both decided they'd skip the fancy dinner and just eat in the hotel dining room, where Charles was finally able to order his catfish sandwich. They had collected reams of materials on things to do and had decided to choose one or two activities for the next day and then come back to the hotel to rest up for their evening cruise.

They both fell asleep not long after dinner and slept until early morning. Sarah woke up first and called down for coffee and bagels. Charles was just waking up when the food arrived, and Sarah was coming out of the shower. "Good morning, sleepyhead," she said as she wrapped her wet hair in a towel.

"What's this?" Charles asked, eyeing the pastry.

"It's called a *beignet*. The woman at the desk told me about it when I called down for coffee and bagels. She said this is a traditional New Orleans pastry, sort of like an English fritter. It's fried and coated with confectioners' sugar."

"It tastes like a donut, only much better," Charles remarked as he savored his first bite. "But they put cream in my coffee ..."

"She also recommended we have café au lait with the beignets."

"Whatever the desk lady says," he commented. "She obviously knows what she's talking about."

After they had eaten, Charles pulled out their tourist materials, and after much deliberation, they finally settled on a couple of ideas. Sarah was interested in the New Orleans Museum of Art, and Charles' vote was for the National World War II Museum, although he knew his wife wasn't going to be interested in his choice. Before she had a chance to object, he quickly suggested that they take the streetcar all the way up to City Park, where the art museum was located, and he'd take a cab back to the WWII museum. "Then we'll meet at City Park for lunch. In fact, if I see a deli, I'll bring lunch, and we'll picnic in the park."

Their plans almost changed when they arrived at the park and were overwhelmed by its beauty. Branches of centuries-old oaks intertwined and hung to the ground, providing a shady shelter for visitors. There were lakes with waterfowl, rowboats, and footbridges, and gardens with expanses of green grass and gazebos. "A perfect place for a wedding," Sarah said. "I think I could easily spend the entire day right here."

But after a peaceful stroll, they decided to stick with their original plans. Charles walked Sarah to the gallery entrance and headed for the main street to hail a cab. Once he entered the war museum, he completely lost track of time. Exhibits included letters, diaries, and photographs; weapons;

and oral histories. There were three buildings focused on different aspects of the war. Charles was a history buff but was particularly intrigued by the details of World War II. It occurred during his early childhood, but he was old enough to sense the concern among his family and friends.

As Charles viewed and interacted with the displays, he found himself transported to another time and place. He found it difficult to pull himself out of it when he realized he'd been there three hours and it was past time to meet his wife. After experiencing the emotions triggered by the displays, he looked forward to the serenity he would feel in the park and in the presence of his wife. As it wasn't far, Charles walked back to the park, totally forgetting to watch for a delicatessen.

Approaching the museum entrance, he was pleased to see Sarah just coming down the marble steps. She, too, had become lost in the exhibits. They decided to take the streetcar back across town and hop off when they spotted an interesting area for lunch.

"Let's get off here," Charles announced suddenly, pulling the cord. "I see a grill that looks inviting, and it has outside seating." As they approached the restaurant, they saw a large sign that said they featured muffulettas. "We have to get that," Charles said excitedly. "It's tradition."

"What is it exactly?"

"It's some kind of sandwich, but I don't know what's on it. I just know that two of our patrolmen came to us from Louisiana, and they bragged that it was the best sandwich you can get anywhere."

Although comfortable earlier in the day, the city was heating up as the day went on, and Sarah suggested they eat inside where it would be cool. Once they were seated, Charles ordered them each a mug of Abita Amber, which the waitress assured him was a staple in New Orleans. "Although it's brewed across the river from us," she had said, "we claim it as our own."

"Could you tell me about the muffuletta?" Sarah asked, feeling embarrassed that she had to ask. "We're from out of town ..." she started to explain, but the waitress just nodded and said that most of their customers were.

"It's a large round sandwich on muffuletta bread. It's filled with olive salad, mortadella, salami, ham, mozzarella, and provolone. The bread is sesame crusted and soft on the inside. It's quite big, and many customers split it. Or you can order just a half if you prefer. Actually," she added, just above a whisper, "There's one being served now at the table next to you."

Sarah and Charles discreetly glanced over, and their eyes grew big at the sight. It stood at least six inches high with layer after layer of meats, cheeses, and what was obviously the olive salad.

"That looks fantastic," Sarah responded. "Do you want a whole one?" she asked, turning to Charles, "Or shall we split one?"

"Let's split it, and maybe we'll have room for dessert," he added, giving Sarah a mischievous look.

It arrived cut in quarters, along with two plates. "It's as big as a cake!" Sarah exclaimed. As it turned out, Sarah could barely finish one of the quarters, and by the time Charles finished the other three-quarters and a second mug of Abita Amber, he couldn't even think about dessert.

Fortunately, by the time they got home, they still had three hours until the steamboat left the dock. They had reservations for 8:00, which left them time to relax before their next and final adventure. Charles sat down and thumbed through the local telephone directory while Sarah stretched out on the bed. She was asleep within moments. Charles quietly stood up and tore a piece of paper out of his notebook. He quickly wrote, "Back soon. Charles."

Chapter 18

"What time is your flight?" Sophie asked when Sarah called her the next morning from the airport.

"We don't leave for another hour, but Charles wanted us to be all checked in well in advance. He's eager to get home, and I can see that Maud is tired. She said she had a fantastic time with her cousin, but it wore them both out."

"I'm glad you called me," Sophie said. "I haven't wanted to call and interrupt your vacation, but Timmy told me that you know about his job at the fire station."

"Yes. Martha called and was very excited."

"So is Timmy, but I thought it was too much of a coincidence that this offer came right when it did. I'm wondering if Charles had anything to do with it."

"I'm sure he got the job on his own. Your son will be a tremendous asset to the department and will give the fire chief a chance to be with his wife. She's very sick, you know."

"I didn't know. What's wrong with her?"

Sarah smiled, knowing that she had skillfully moved her friend off of the original question. She didn't want to lie to her, yet she didn't want to betray Charles' confidence. She went on to tell Sophie about the fire chief's wife, and they discussed talking to the members of the quilt club about making her a quilt as a thank-you for her years of community service. Chief Deegan's wife had continued her community volunteer work long after she had been diagnosed with Parkinson's.

Before Sophie could get back to the fire station issue, Sarah said, "I can't wait to tell you about the dinner cruise we took last night."

"Well, you can tell me about that when you get home. Right now I want to ask you about Tim's job …"

"And there's something else," Sarah whispered, looking around to be sure Charles wasn't near. "Yesterday while I was napping, Charles snuck out of the hotel room and was gone for at least an hour, maybe longer."

"That's strange," Sophie replied. "Maybe he was buying you a present."

"No, it wasn't that."

"How do you know?"

"Because he was very distracted the rest of the evening. All evening it was as if his mind was somewhere else, the way he acts when he's on a case."

"Did you ask him where he went?"

"Yes, but he just said …" Sarah stopped talking abruptly, then added, "Here he comes. I don't want him to hear me talking about this. I will be home soon and will come see you in the morning."

"Who's on the phone?" Charles asked cheerfully as he walked up.

"Sophie, just saying hello."

Within another twenty minutes, their flight was announced. They were eligible for early boarding since

Maud was in a wheelchair. It took some convincing, but she finally agreed. "I'm bone-tired," she said, "and I suppose I can do it this once."

Once they were settled in their seats, Maud asked what Sarah and Charles did while they were there, and together they told her about their sightseeing and the extraordinary food. Sarah told her that the very best part of the whole experience was the riverboat cruise. "They served dinner in five separate courses," she said, "and I tried everything, whether I recognized it or not."

"And it was wonderful, wasn't it?" Maud exclaimed.

"It was. Had you been there before?" Sarah asked, realizing it had never occurred to her that she might be familiar with the area since she had family living there.

"When I was much younger, I visited Bessie a couple of times after she married Bertram and moved down there. I mostly remember the food, and I sure got some while I was there this time. Her grandson, Gilbert, is a chef at a restaurant down by the river, and he brought home food from his kitchen. I love New Orleans cookin'. Did you folks get any jambalaya?"

"As a matter of fact, we did. It was one of our courses on the riverboat. Oh, and the music. I never knew I liked jazz, but I learned to love it in one night!"

"You just hadn't heard the real thing," Maud responded with a chuckle.

Sarah noticed how relaxed Maud seemed now that the trip was winding down. "Are you glad you came?" Sarah asked her.

"I wouldn't have missed this for the world, no matter how it comes out."

* * * * *

They arrived home late that night, and Sarah considered ignoring the flashing lights on the house phone but decided that wondering about the calls might keep her awake. "You go ahead and pick up Barney," she said to Charles, "and I'll at least see who these calls are from."

When he arrived back with an excited Barney in tow, Charles knew right away that Sarah was upset. "What is it?"

"You have three calls from that detective in New Orleans and one from your old lieutenant here in Middletown, and both men sounded upset. They both want you to call right away, and both said you weren't answering your cell phone."

"Oops," he responded, pulling the phone out of his pocket. "I turned it off at the airport and forgot all about it." He went into his computer room to listen to the messages on his cell phone and on the house phone. He looked at the clock and decided he should, at least, call his lieutenant. "Matt, sorry to call so late but we just got in."

Without acknowledging Charles, Lieutenant Stokely demanded to know what was going on. "Why am I getting calls from New Orleans charging that this department is interfering in a murder investigation, and why do they specifically name you as the Middletown detective doing the interfering?"

"Matt, let me explain. I didn't mean to bring the department into it, but I did leave my card with a couple of people. They must have reported it. I was just doing some snooping for a friend."

"Well, for one thing, you need to get rid of those department cards and get yourself some *Private Snooper* cards. I don't want this to happen again. What were you doing anyway?"

Charles explained about Jamal and why they were in New Orleans. "At the request of the New Orleans police department's prosecutor, I might add." He told Matt about Jamal's second wife's accidental death and that he was just doing some snooping around in the neighborhood. "I wanted to talk to a couple of neighbors to see what kind of marriage they had."

"Which is none of our business," Lieutenant Stokely responded.

"I know, Matt, but I just have a feeling that everyone is missing something here."

"And this is your concern why?"

"I guess it's not, but you know how hard it is to leave something alone when it's niggling at you."

Lieutenant Stokely was quiet for a few moments. "I know how hard it is for you, Charles, but I can't keep reminding you that you're retired, and you can't represent yourself as a member of the department. Do you want to get yourself a PI license? If you do, I'll back you."

"It's something to think about, Matt. Thanks, and I'm sorry to cause you problems. I'll get this straightened out with New Orleans."

"I hope you can. Good night, Charlie." Although Charles didn't like being called Charlie, he had to smile when Matt used it at the end of the conversation, knowing that it meant Matt had already forgiven him.

"So that's what this is all about." Sarah's voice behind him caused him to jump and almost drop the phone.

"I was going to tell you."

Sarah signed and walked away. *There's no way I will ever get him to stop being a detective. I give up*, she told herself firmly.

Before she had reached the bedroom, she heard his cell phone ring again. "Mrs. Carlson, thank you for calling me. My name is Detective Parker. I'm a private investigator out of Illinois, and I'm looking into the death of Angela Davis. I understand you two were friends, and I was hoping you could tell me a little about the Davis' relationship." Sarah moved back up the hall and stood in the doorway. She wanted him to see her so he wouldn't think she was snooping. She, in fact, wondered whether Jamal's second wife had suffered the pain and humiliation that Clarissa had experienced.

There was a long silence, occasionally punctuated by comments from Charles like, "I see," and "Please go on." After ten or fifteen minutes, Sarah went up the hall to her bedroom and unpacked their bag. When Charles finally came into the room, he looked exhausted.

"I take it she had a great deal to say," Sarah commented in a neutral tone. Actually, she was very curious about what he had learned and hoped he would volunteer it.

"Would you like to hear about it?" He wasn't sure how upset she was, but from the look of curiosity on her face, he decided she must be over her initial reaction.

"She didn't say anything I expected her to say."

"How's that?" Sarah sat down on the bed and patted the seat next to her, indicating he should sit as well. They were both exhausted from their trip.

"She never saw any indication that there could be problems in their marriage. She said they were very much in love and that he doted on her. She described him as a kind and caring man."

"Are we sure we're talking about the same person?"

"Yes. I'd already confirmed that. I asked about his drinking, and she laughed. She said she never saw him take a drink and that Angela had told her he had attended Alcoholics Anonymous twice a week since before they were married. They were next-door neighbors, and she and Angela were friends for over ten years. She said her own husband and Jamal were in a bowling league together, and she and Angela did volunteer work at the local food bank. I got the feeling it would have been impossible to hide it from the Carlsons if anything was going on. The two couples were very close."

"This is strange, but I guess people change. If the alcohol was the main problem with Jamal, perhaps he got into treatment."

"Something sure happened," Charles replied, "but getting his life together doesn't excuse him from killing Clarissa. I feel like we owe it to Maud to pursue this. If what Mrs. Carlson says is true, chances are he's not going to be charged with Angela's death."

"Are you going to call that detective in New Orleans?"

"Not tonight. He just wants to ream me out. He can do that tomorrow. Matt knows the story now. Let's go to bed."

Chapter 19

"So are you any closer to knowing who made the *Memories* quilt?" Sophie asked as she poured their coffee and pulled the freshly baked cinnamon rolls out of the oven.

"Actually, we've become so sidetracked that I'm not even sure where we are with that project."

"Well, I can refresh your memory from my cards here." Sophie pulled out her 3″ by 5″ cards and quickly rearranged them. "Okay, so you bought the quilt from Florence's thrift shop."

She laid that card aside and picked up another one. "Florence got it from the wife of a construction worker who found it in the attic of a building they were tearing down."

"Yes," Sarah said, amused with Sophie's system. "Go on."

"So, you found out that the last person to live in that house was Maud Templeton, and she told you that she was the one who put the quilt in the attic. She said she got the quilt from her grandsons, Jerome and Darnell, now in prison, who stole it from a burning house."

"Yes. And the owner of that house never lived in it so it wasn't his." Sarah added. "He rented it out to a family named ..." She hesitated.

"Anderson," Sophie quickly filled in. "Susan and Phillip Anderson."

"And where did they get it?" Sarah asked, already knowing the answer but enjoying Sophie's enthusiasm.

"They got it as a wedding present from Susan's sister, Marilee, in 1966," Sophie responded, reading from another card.

"And they weren't at all happy about that," Sarah added as an aside.

"No, they weren't, but that doesn't get us anywhere," Sophie responded with a dismissive gesture. "The important point is the name of the sister that gave it to them, and I have that right here." She reached for another card and read, "Marilee, now dead, and her husband, Harry, gave Susan and Phillip the quilt, but I don't seem to have their last name," she added, fumbling through her cards.

"Wilkinson, I think," Sarah suggested tentatively at first, but then added, "Yes, Marilee Wilkinson. She gave the quilt to the Andersons as a wedding present, and Marilee got it from an elderly friend of hers named Agatha Tarkington, as I remember."

"That's right," Sophie said, laying aside her last card. "Agatha Tarkington may have been the last family member to own the quilt. Marilee's husband stated that Agatha didn't have any children or siblings to pass it on to, but she told Marilee that it was a family heirloom."

"Okay," Sarah said, reaching for a cinnamon bun. "That answers your question about where we are with the search."

"It does, but that's where we were two weeks ago," Sophie responded. "We aren't making any progress."

"And that's primarily because Charles got sidetracked. Meeting Maud Templeton and hearing about the sad death of her daughter got him distracted from his computer searches, and I think we're going to have to take that over."

"Why? What's he going to be doing?"

"He's determined to find some kind of closure for Maud. Certainly testifying in New Orleans helped her, but Charles doesn't think the grand jury is going to indict Jamal, and that's going to leave Maud right where she was when we met her."

"Didn't you tell me you have a friend who knows how to do ancestor searches? We're not looking for living people any longer. We're looking for Agatha Tarkington's ancestors."

"True, and that's an excellent point. I'll give my friend Paula a call and see if she'll talk with us about the next steps. She has her ancestors tracked back to the sixteenth century. Surely she can tell us where to go from here."

"Good plan," Sophie responded. "And there's one card here which is still marked pending, and that's the one about the Tarkington wing in City Hospital."

"Oh my!" Sarah exclaimed. "Ruth told me about that the night before we left for New Orleans, and I completely forgot about it!"

"You can tell your husband to stop making fun of my 3″ by 5″ cards," Sophie responded, "because, as you can plainly see, they just saved the day!"

"You are so right. Thank you, Sophie. I'll call the hospital administrator tomorrow and see what I can find out."

"Now for the strange disappearance of your husband on the last day of your getaway. You were starting to tell me about that when he walked up at the airport."

Sarah caught Sophie up on Charles' detective adventure in New Orleans, and they agreed that the best thing to do was to stay out of it and let Charles make his own decisions about how far he wanted to go. "It's who he is," Sarah had said, and Sophie agreed.

Sarah had brought Barney with her. Sophie and Sarah decided to put ice cubes in the leftover coffee and take iced coffee and the dogs into the backyard so they could play. Once they were seated in Sophie's new padded lounge chairs, Sarah told her friend about the sightseeing they had done, the evening cruise, and the exquisite food they had enjoyed.

Sophie wanted all the details on jambalaya and asked Sarah to find her a recipe online that sounded authentic. "I'll make it for the six of us this weekend."

"Six?" Sarah repeated quickly, counting only five. "You invited Charles and me, Timothy and Martha, and there's you.… Oh, I forgot Penny."

"Penny is going to be spending the night with Caitlyn," Sophie responded. "This is grown-ups night."

"So who's the sixth person?" Sarah asked, tilting her head and raising an eyebrow when she noticed that Sophie's cheeks were a bit flushed.

"Just a person I met at the senior center," Sophie said, dropping her eyes. "It's nothing," she quickly added. "I just thought he'd like a home-cooked meal."

"That's sweet of you, but it hardly justifies the rosy color in your cheeks. Who is this man?"

"We'll talk about that another time," Sophie said with a wave of her hand, firmly declaring an end to the discussion. "Just get me that recipe."

Before Sarah left, Sophie said she wanted to show her the progress she'd made on the wedding quilt. "I'm really enjoying this."

When she pulled out her stack of completed hexagons, Sarah was amazed. "How did you get this much done in a couple of weeks? I'm finding each one very time consuming."

"I'm taking the modern shortcuts," Sophie announced proudly, holding up her template and iron-on foundation papers.

"How does that help?" Sarah asked, thinking that just gave her a different template.

"I iron this one onto the back of the fabric and cut it out, leaving the seam allowance. That way it doesn't slip around."

"And you turn the seam allowance and stitch it?"

"Nope. I turn the seam allowance and swipe this water-soluble glue stick across the edge of the paper, and then I turn back the fabric. And I'm ready to whipstitch them together in no time!"

"But how to you get the papers out? Now they are glued in."

"Ah, that's the magic. This paper and the glue is water soluble. I'll just dunk the block in water for a couple of minutes, and it's ready to go."

"That's amazing. We've come a long way since the early days of paper piecing," Sarah commented as she examined the materials and the results. "This looks really nice, and I love your colors."

"I cheated just a little." She held up the book, and Sarah could see that Sophie had followed the layout and colors of the quilt on the cover. "That way I knew it would look good."

Sophie had asked the members of the quilt club to bring her three-inch strips of their floral fabrics, and she had purchased half-yards of different solids. She used yellow for the middle of each of her rosettes, a solid for the six surrounding pieces, and one of the florals for each of the twelve hexagons in the outer ring. "I was able to get twelve hexagons out of each of the strips the girls brought me, but I'm beginning to run low and thought we could go to Stitches. I can buy quarter yards and get three sets for the outer rings from each one."

"How many more rosettes do you need?"

"I figure I need a total of seventy-six whole rosettes and ten half-rosettes. With the path pieces, that should fit their bed."

Sarah measured one of the completed rosettes and found it to be just short of nine inches across. "Yes, that should be just right if you aren't using a border."

"I'm not. I want just rosettes and the path. I have enough fabric for about seventy of them, so I won't need much more."

"Let's go later this week. Did you check the scrap boxes in her storage room?"

"There weren't any pieces big enough to cut twelve matching hexagons."

"Are you going to have it machine quilted?" Sarah asked. She'd been grappling with that issue herself.

"Yes. I talked to Kimberly about it, and she has an idea for custom quilting it."

"She's getting good at that," Sarah replied.

Later, as she walked home leisurely, giving Barney ample time to sniff along the way, Sarah wondered whether she should switch to the more modern technique of piecing the quilt. *It would certainly take less time*, she told herself. *On the other hand, I'm trying to reproduce my* Memories *quilt, and it was made the original way.*

Whenever Sarah worked on the quilt, she was aware that she felt oddly connected to the woman who created *Memories*. "Yes," she added aloud. "I'm going to stay with the old technique."

Barney turned and looked up at her to see if she had said something that might pertain to him, such as an offer of treats or a trip to the dog park. Realizing she hadn't, he sighed and continued to sniff his way home.

* * * * *

As Sarah stepped into the house, she could hear a loud, angry voice.

"And I don't want you going near Jamal Davis, his son, or his neighbors. Do you get that?" the angry voice demanded. Sarah hurried up the hall, following the sound.

"His son?" Sarah heard her husband respond. He had the phone on speaker and was sitting at his computer when Sarah approached the room. "What son?"

The voice on the phone replied furiously, "Detective Parker, I've said all I intend to say to you on this matter. From this point on, any conversations will be between your lieutenant and mine." The man hung up.

Sarah stepped into the room and started to say something consoling, but her husband had apparently moved past the reprimand.

"Which son is he talking about?" Charles said rhetorically. "Jerome and Darnell are both in prison, right?"

"Yes, but wasn't there another son?" Sarah responded. "I think I remember Maud saying Jamal had a son of his own when he married her daughter."

"You're right, and I remember you asking what happened to the older boy and she didn't know. That son just might know exactly what happened. There's a good chance he could have witnessed it, in fact. Why don't you give her a call and see if she can remember anything about him?"

"I'll call her in the morning," Sarah responded. "I need to call City Hospital as well."

"Couldn't you call her now?" Charles asked, impatient to start tracking the man. It just occurred to him that the older son just might be more than just a witness. *Could he have killed his stepmother?* he wondered but didn't say.

"I suppose I could call her now," Sarah responded with a sigh. "She doesn't go to bed until 8:00. After I talk to her, I'm going to bring some hand sewing into the living room and watch a movie. Do you want to join me?"

"I'll be in later. Just let me know what Maud has to say."

Once Sarah got settled in the living room, she picked up her cell phone and called Maud, but she wasn't able to get any more information than they already had.

"His name is Jackson Davis," Sarah told Charles, "and I remember now that Maud told us that the day we met her. She said he was five or six years old when her daughter married Jamal, which would make him in his late forties now. Maud said she never got to know the child." Maud had told Sarah that Jamal didn't like for her to visit their house and when Clarissa would bring the boys to visit her, she never brought Jackson.

"So she has no idea what became of him?"

"No idea," Sarah responded.

"With the history the other boys have, he's probably known to the criminal justice system. I'll check that out now."

When Charles emerged from his computer room an hour later, he looked glum. "No luck," he announced. "I even checked the national system. He's never been arrested anywhere."

"Sounds like he didn't follow in the family's footsteps," Sarah responded.

"Or he never got caught," Charles responded, sounding disappointed. Charles sighed and glanced at the television screen. "How's the movie?" he asked.

"I figured you'd be a while, so I chose a romantic comedy. I don't think you'd like it, and it's almost over anyway." Sarah moved her project aside so Charles could sit down next to her. He appeared to be watching the last twenty minutes of the movie, but Sarah knew his mind was on Jamal and on Maud's daughter.

Once the movie ended, Sarah turned to her husband. "Did that neighbor who called you say anything about Jamal having a son?"

"Mrs. Carlson? No, as a matter of fact. She only referred to the couple, Jamal and Angela."

'Hmm." She took a few stitches in her hexagons and then laid the project down in her lap and looked at her husband. "You have a plan, don't you?"

"I do."

Sarah sighed. "And?"

"I'm going to find Jackson Davis."

Chapter 20

"I can't take all the credit," Sophie was saying as she scooped jambalaya into everyone's bowl. "I couldn't have done it without Sarah's recipe."

"It looks just like what we had in New Orleans," Charles remarked as he watched the andouille sausage rounds, chicken breast pieces, shrimp, tomatoes, diced peppers, and rice being heaped into his bowl. Sophie added a scoop of the broth, which was still steaming.

"You've been to New Orleans?" Sophie's guest asked. He had simply been introduced as Norman Hill, a gentleman she met at the senior center. Charles gave him a brief rundown on the trip, excluding the hearing, and Sarah interjected some of the high points, including the cruise where they were introduced to jambalaya.

"I worked briefly in New Orleans some fifty years ago," Mr. Hill offered, confirming Sarah's thought that the man must be at least in his seventies, if not older. He wasn't much taller than Sophie and was very attentive to her, helping her with her chair and frequently glancing her way during dinner.

Timothy and Martha sat opposite Sarah and Charles while Sophie and Norman Hill sat at each end of the table.

Charles asked Tim about his job. He had already started working with Deegan and was eager to talk about it. "You know what my first task was, don't you?" he asked, looking at Charles with a grin.

"Not the Quonset hut, I hope."

"You guessed it. My first assignment is to get that stuff in some kind of order and work with a contract company that will do the data entry."

Charles laughed. "Well, we left it in better shape than we found it."

Mr. Hill, acknowledging that Sophie had told him that Timothy was retired from the pipeline, asked him about his experiences in Alaska. That led to a lively discussion about the Keystone pipeline controversy.

"Charles here," Timothy began, hoping to get out of the limelight, "is the one with the most impressive career. He was a detective with Middletown Police Department for … what, Charles? Thirty years?"

"Yep."

"And I'll bet he loved every minute of it," Martha interjected. "Mom says he's a detective at heart."

Charles, looking self-conscious said, "Let's not bore this gentleman with my escapades. How about you, Mr. Hill? What career did you leave behind?"

"Well, first of all, call me Norman. And I didn't really leave it behind. I still get involved from time to time. I own Top of the Hill," he announced proudly, assuming everyone would know what it was.

"I'm not familiar with Top of the Hill. What do they do?" Charles asked.

"We are wedding planners."

Martha shot a harsh look at her mother, but Sarah merely shrugged her shoulders and shook her head, indicating she knew nothing about it. Martha looked at Tim, who turned his eyes on Sophie.

"Mother?" he began in a reproachful voice.

"What, dear?" Sophie responded innocently.

"What are you up to?" he demanded, slamming his napkin down on the table. "You know what Martha and I told you …"

"I know, I know," she responded. "I just wanted you to meet Norman. He's been talking to me about some of the pitfalls of planning your own wedding, and I thought you might like to meet him. He offered to answer any questions you two might have. Believe me, I'm not trying to interfere."

"Not much you aren't," Timothy snapped.

"Your mother's right," Norman spoke up, looking directly at Timothy. "It was my idea. I offered to answer any questions you two might have, and your mother suggested we have dinner together. As you know, your mother and I have been seeing one another for several months now, and I've been eager to meet the rest of the family."

Everyone stopped eating, several with their forks in the air. For a few moments there was no response, until finally Charles spoke up, saying, "I think I can speak for everyone here when I say that we're all very happy to meet you, Mr. Hill."

"Please," he repeated. "It's Norman."

"Yes," Sarah said, "We're delighted to finally meet you." When Norman Hill wasn't looking, she shot her friend a look which clearly said that Sophie had some explaining to do.

Everyone resumed eating but avoided each other's eyes. Sophie passed the corn bread around again, and Charles stood to refill everyone's wine glass with the Riesling Spatlese. At this point, he was relieved that he had brought several bottles.

"How did you decide to become a wedding planner?" Sarah asked in an attempt to defuse the tension at the table.

"Just luck, I guess," Mr. Hill responded. "My early experience was in advertising. The company I was with had downsized, and we began doubling up on jobs. The task that was passed to me was event planning—conferences, training, and special occasions. I discovered that I got a real kick out of pulling all the details together, and especially when I could see people enjoying themselves, and I started thinking about going into business for myself. I had some money saved up and was able to get a small business loan, and that was the beginning of Top of the Hill. Hill, get it?"

"Ah," Sarah nodded. "Norman Hill—Top of the Hill."

"Right!"

"And I had a great time for the next thirty years. It was always exciting, always a challenge. I had brides that changed their minds and grooms that didn't show up. I had a pet pig for a ring bearer once and a ceremony on a ski sloop. You just have to roll with the punches," he added, laughing. "Most of the time I was blissfully happy meeting the needs of rooms filled with joyful people."

"It sounds like you enjoyed your work," Sarah commented.

"I did, and I guess that's why I haven't been able to completely let it go. I have good people running it, but I just need to get in there from time to time. I'm sure they wish I'd stay home."

"That's about what my ex-boss said to me just yesterday," Charles said with an understanding chuckle. "They want us old guys to stay in the pasture."

Toward the end of the meal, Martha asked, "Does Top of the Hill only plan weddings?" She was thinking about her company's national conference that was a year away, but she had volunteered to play an instrumental part in the planning.

"Oh, no. I immediately branched out into planning corporate events, conferences, and social events, but where I felt most at home was with weddings—the emotions, the happiness, the excitement, and oh so many details!"

"And you still own the company?" Martha asked. Tim wondered why Martha seemed so interested considering she was the one that insisted they plan their own wedding.

"I do, and as I said, I still get involved, but in general I'm retired. Do you have a need for an event coordinator?" he asked, confused by her sudden interest in light of her original reaction.

"Not me personally," she responded emphatically, "but my company may well need your services."

Norman Hill passed her his card just as Sophie stood and said, "Anyone for bread pudding with whiskey sauce? I've been told it goes perfectly after a meal of jambalaya." She winked at Sarah, who had included the recipe when she brought the one for the main dish.

Sophie's guests were practically moaning as they spooned up the incredible dessert. "Sophie, this is scrumptious," Sarah said, and everyone nodded their agreement but weren't willing to stop eating to comment.

As they were leaving, Sarah noticed that Sophie and Martha were whispering at the door. Then they hugged, and Martha kissed her future mother-in-law on the cheek. Sarah was glad to see that they were growing close, but she was baffled about this relationship with Norman. *Why didn't she tell me?* Sarah wondered.

As they were walking home, Charles asked if Sarah knew that Sophie was seeing Norman Hill.

"I had no idea, and I'm eager to hear why she's kept this a secret. Apparently no one at that table knew about it. All I know is that she met him at the Community Center."

"I'll see what I can find out about him," Charles responded before thinking and was immediately sorry he had said it.

"Charles. Don't you dare start investigating our friends."

* * * * *

"So what do you have planned for today?" Charles asked as they were finishing their breakfast.

"I'm hoping for a quiet morning in the sewing room," Sarah responded. "Then this afternoon, Sophie and I are going to meet with my friend Paula. She's agreed to show us how to research Agatha Tarkington's family tree. How about you?"

"I'm going to take a chance and call that neighbor Mrs. Carlson again. She was very forthcoming with her information and seemed to be a real friend of the Davis'.

I don't think she's the one that reported me to the cops down there. I want to ask her about the son."

"What's the worst that can happen?" Sarah asked.

"I get reamed out again. I'm tough. I can take it." He joshed.

"Yeah, you're one tough guy alright. Now, put that kitty cat down and go take your pills."

Charles sat Bootsy on the floor, and she immediately ran over and jumped on Barney, who had been peacefully sleeping in the corner of the room. He made a short warning yip, and within seconds Bootsy was back on top of the kitchen cabinets where she had made her home.

Chapter 21

"Let me take a look at what you have and I'll see what I can do."

Sophie and Sarah were sitting in Paula's kitchen with Sophie's 3″ by 5″ cards spread out on the table. Paula had been tracking her own family history in great detail for years, and Sarah felt confident she would be able to get them going in the right direction.

As Sophie read aloud from her cards, with Sarah interjecting her own comments now and then, Paula made notes on a legal pad and occasionally asked for clarification. This continued for over an hour until finally Sophie sighed and said, "Okay, that's as far as we've gotten."

Paula studied her legal pad for a few minutes and then got up and poured them each another cup of coffee. "It seems to me that I saw the name Tarkington the last time I was at City Hospital. It's a wing or something …"

"Oh, I'm sorry. I forgot to tell you about that," Sarah responded. "I called the hospital administrator about that. Agatha arranged for a sizable endowment for the hospital when she died. He wasn't able to give me much information about it, but he referred me to her attorney."

"Was he any help?" Sophie asked, looking irritated, and Sarah immediately realized she'd forgotten to fill Sophie in on that call.

"No, but it was apparent that he didn't have any information that would be helpful. He did confirm there were no heirs, and he said all of her assets went to charitable organizations, with the bulk being the hospital."

"Well," Paula responded, "It looks to me like what you want to know is who passed the quilt to Agatha Tarkington for safekeeping. And since she said it was a family heirloom, I assume we want to know who her parents were first of all, and if there were siblings, right?"

"We were told there were no siblings, but that probably should be confirmed."

"Do you want to do this research yourselves?" Paula asked. "I can give you some pointers to get you started if you'd like."

"I have a computer, and I could probably do it," Sarah responded reluctantly. "But …"

"Or," Paula added, "I'd be happy to do some preliminary searches for you."

"I hate to trouble you, Paula, but if you're willing to take a look at it, we'd appreciate it. Sophie and I have no experience with this sort of thing, and I don't think my husband does either, although he's great on the computer."

"Okay. How about this," Paula suggested. "I'll take a look at the census reports and the ancestry databases and see if I can identify Agatha's parents, and we'll see where that takes us."

Sarah and Sophie left Paula's house feeling elated. "We're making some progress," Sophie commented as they drove off.

"I think so," Sarah responded, but she wondered just what good it would do to learn the names of ancestors unless there was also information about their quilts, which of course the databases wouldn't include.

"Do we have time to stop at the house before Delores' class?" Sophie asked. "I forgot to bring my hexagons."

"How's your quilt coming?"

"It's coming along. I sure hope I can get this done by September. I probably took on too much."

"Didn't you tell me you're putting a white path between your rosettes?"

"Yes, that's what the pattern says to do. Why?"

"Would you like for me to cut your white hexagons and start basting them to their templates?"

"I'd love that, Sarah," Sophie exclaimed, "but remember, I'm not sewing them on; I'm using temporary glue."

"That's fine. I could even start whipstitching some of them in strips if you show me your pattern."

"Sarah, that would be such a big help," Sophie gushed, a tone she rarely exhibited." Her tone changed somewhat when she remembered Sarah's project. "But aren't you busy with your own project?" Sarah had purchased several scrap bags of 1800s reproduction fabrics for her *Memories* project. Although she was attempting to reproduce it as closely as possible, the resulting quilt top appeared different due to the new, crisp, and undamaged fabrics.

"It's coming along. There's no hurry. I just work on it when I have free time. That's what I love about the English paper piecing—I can work on it anywhere. I went to the doctor with Charles yesterday and sat for an hour working on it."

"Is Charles okay?"

"This was a routine visit, but we had planned to do some shopping afterward, so I just went with him since it's so easy to entertain myself now."

At the meeting later that night, Delores helped the class complete their table toppers and used Sophie's project as a tool for demonstrating the newer techniques. She also brought in samples of some of her own very modern versions of hexagons, which were constructed using several other shapes and various colors within each hexagon. The group was enthralled, but no one felt ready to suggest she teach that class.

On their way home, Sarah and Sophie agreed to meet at Sophie's house early the next morning to set up a workspace in her spare room so they could begin working together on the wedding quilt. "I'll have Charles drop me off, and he can bring one of those worktables from the garage."

* * * * *

"Mrs. Carlson, this is Charles Parker. I'm …"

"Oh, I remember you, Detective. You're the policeman that talked to me about Jamal and his wife."

"Actually, Mrs. Carlson, I'm a retired police officer from up north, and I'm trying to help out a friend."

"I wondered what was going on. A local detective came by and asked me all about your visit. I told him I had no problem talking with you, but he seemed upset. Now I understand," she added with a chuckle.

"Yeah," he responded. "It's a jurisdictional thing. Anyway, would you mind answering just one more question for me?"

"Detective Parker, I'd be happy to answer any question you have. Angela and Jamal were our closest friends, and I miss her so much."

"How's Jamal doing?" he asked, still curious about the man's changed behavior.

"He's doing pretty well. He told my husband that he's going to meetings every day now, and he has dinner with us two or three times a week. I know he's grieving, but he's handling it. He's planning to stay on here. I thought he might want to sell the house with all its memories, but he said he feels at home here, and it's got plenty of room for when his son visits."

"His son? Actually, that's why I was calling."

"I don't think we talked about Jackson when we spoke before. He's such a nice young man. Actually, he's probably approaching fifty, but everyone under sixty seems young to me," she added with another chuckle.

"So he visits Jamal? Do you know where he lives?"

"He went back to live in his hometown, as far as I know," she responded.

I keep doing this, Charles chastised himself. He had assumed that since Jamal took his son with him when he left Middletown, the son never returned. *It never occurred to me that Jackson might be right here. I'm slowing down. Maybe Sarah is right when she says I'm getting too old for this kind of work.*

Forcing himself back to their conversation, he asked a few questions about the son's visits. He learned that Jackson was a teacher in Middletown. "He teaches high school, I think.

He said they are a pretty rough bunch of kids, but he loves working with them. He's a really nice young man."

As they ended their conversation, Mrs. Carlson encouraged Charles to call back if he had any other questions.

After he hung up the phone, Charles remained sitting at his desk, staring at the few notes he had made.

Why didn't I think of this? All I had to do was check with Motor Vehicles. I wonder if those strokes have affected my mind? He didn't want to ask Sarah because he didn't want to admit that he was having problems, and he didn't want to worry her. *I'll talk to the doctor about it*, he assured himself.

Picking up the phone again, he called his contact at Motor Vehicles and a few minutes later had Jackson Davis' address and phone number. With a few more computer searches, he had Jackson's resume, which had been submitted to the school board, and the names of other people living in his household: a Phyllis Davis, forty-seven, and a daughter, Adrianna, thirteen. He also found reference to two books coauthored by Jackson Davis for sale on a textbook website.

"Okay," Charles said aloud. "Not bad research for an old man!"

Chapter 22

The next morning, Charles called Dr. Grossman's office to make an appointment. The doctor had a cancellation, and the receptionist told him to come on in. Charles made another call before leaving and made an appointment with his old lieutenant, Matthew Stokely.

"What's this all about?" Stokely had asked, still a bit peeved with Charles.

"I'll explain when I get there," Charles assured him.

Sarah had left early that morning to help Sophie with her quilt. He left her a note saying that he had some stops to make and would see her later. He didn't explain beyond that.

He drove directly to the doctor's office and was feeling nervous when he sat down across the desk from the doctor who had seen him through his original stroke and had continued treating him since that time. He had told the receptionist he didn't need an examination, that he just wanted to talk with the doctor about a personal problem.

"I'm worried about my mind, doctor."

"Your mind?" The doctor seemed surprised. "You're one of the sharpest men I know, Charles. What's your concern?"

Charles told him about the few details he had missed here and there over the past year, and a couple of times when he had forgotten someone's name or couldn't find something he had misplaced. "I'm worried that my mind is going," he said.

"Charles, what you're experiencing is what we all experience as we get older. Forgetting is perfectly normal at our age." Charles knew the doctor was at least fifteen years younger than he was, but he appreciated being including in the physician's age range. "What I tell my patients is that if you forget where you put your car keys, that's perfectly normal. If you don't know what your car keys are for, that may be problematic."

"But all those strokes?"

The doctor smiled and replied, "Are you forgetting about all those tests? I've seen your brain from every possible angle. You showed no signs of permanent damage, and you worked very hard in rehab to regain the losses you did suffer back then. And just remember, Charles, you only had one serious stroke, and that was nearly ten years ago. The other one you had out in Tennessee was just a warning, and from what I can see, you've heeded the warning."

"Sarah has heeded the warning," Charles corrected him with an appreciative smile.

"Stop worrying, Charles. You are right where you should be."

Charles took a deep breath and thanked the doctor for his time.

He headed for the police station with renewed enthusiasm and feeling about twenty years younger.

"Go on back," the desk sergeant said as Charles walked into the station. "He's expecting you."

"Matt," Charles said, reaching out to shake his friend's hand. "Thanks for seeing me on such short notice."

"Happy to, Charlie. So what's going on?"

Charles went over his concerns about Jamal and his first wife's death. He could see Matt Stokely's reluctance to get involved, but when Charles got to the part about locating the older son and his speculation that the son might have witnessed her death, or even participated in it, he showed more interest. "What is it you want to do?"

"I want to interview him."

Stokely sat silently, apparently thinking about what Charles had told him. Finally he spoke up, saying, "I reviewed that case last week after your exploits in Louisiana ..."

Charles shrugged his apology.

"And I can see why you'd have questions. Let's see if this Jackson Davis will come in and talk to us. We have no basis for bringing him in, but he might be willing to come in on his own."

"Will you be interviewing him yourself?" Charles asked, hoping to be involved but reluctant to ask.

"You've got a way with these guys, Charlie. You go see him and ask him to come in. You can do the interview, but I'd like to sit in. I'll put you on the books just for this limited assignment." He stressed the last sentence, letting Charles know he wasn't giving him free reign.

"Thanks, Matt. I understand the limitations."

"I hope so," Stokely replied, attempting to look stern but appreciating his friend's diligence and skill.

* * * * *

"Did you get your project finished with Sophie?" he asked when Sarah walked in a few hours after his return. She was carrying a tote bag filled with white fabric, which she sat down on the kitchen table. She pulled out a handful of white fabric hexagons. "It's far from finished," Sarah responded. "But this is my contribution to Sophie's wedding quilt for the kids. It's going to be beautiful."

"It's all white?" he said, looking hesitant.

"Oh no, it's very colorful. We'll bring it over for you to see when we get farther along. This is just my small contribution. What have you been doing today?" she asked, picking up the note he had left her.

Leaving out the appointment with Dr. Grossman, he told her about his phone call the previous evening with Mrs. Carlson and what he had learned about Jackson. Then he told her about his visit with Matt and that he had a very limited contract with the department to do two things: attempt to get Jackson to agree to an interview at the department and to conduct that interview to see what he might know about Clarissa's death.

"What if he killed her?" Sarah asked. It was a question he had in his own mind, but he didn't realize she had considered it as well.

"Then I guess he won't agree to come in."

"And you'll leave it at that?" she asked, looking doubtful.

"I haven't been authorized go any farther. So, yes, I'll leave it at that. Of course, Matt might decide to pursue it," he added and saw his wife frown.

"I want to get started on these hexagons," Sarah said, changing the subject. "Would soup and sandwiches be okay for dinner?"

"That would be fine," he responded, relieved that she was willing to drop the subject for now.

* * * * *

The next morning, Charles placed a call to East Middletown High School and asked for Jackson Davis. He was told that Mr. Davis was in class. Charles left a message for him to return the call at his convenience. Within the hour, Jackson called.

"Mr. Davis, thank you for returning my call. I'm a detective working with the Middletown Police Department. I'm wondering if I could arrange an appointment to meet with you."

"What's this about?" Jackson asked cautiously.

"The department has been reviewing cold cases, and we'd like to ask you a few questions about the death of your stepmother, Clarissa Davis."

"Good Lord, detective. That really is a cold case! Clarissa's been gone for over thirty years!"

"I know. It came to our attention recently …"

"When Dad's second wife died, I assume," Jackson interjected. "When are you folks going to leave my dad alone?" Charles thought the man was preparing to terminate the conversation, but instead Jackson said, "Sure, we can talk. Do you want me to come into the station?"

Charles thought for a second. He had planned to meet with Mr. Davis at the school in order to convince him to come into the station, but it looked like that wasn't going to be necessary. Mr. Davis was already offering to come in.

"I'd appreciate that," Charles responded. "What's a good time for you?"

"How about today? Let's get this over with. My last class is finished at 3:45. I can be there by 4:15."

"That's fine. Just ask for me when you arrive."

Jackson hung up the phone without a word, leaving Charles wondering if he would change his mind about the interview.

He went into the kitchen, where he found Sarah sitting at the table surrounded by white hexagons and a glue stick. "What are you doing?" he asked, picking up one of the completed hexagons. She explained about the foundation paper she had ironed onto the back of the hexagon and showed him how she was gluing the seam allowance under and finger-pressing a sharp edge. She reached for the pile she had whipstitched together the previous evening so he could see the finished product.

"Interesting," he said, although she questioned just how interesting he actually found it. He seemed very distracted, and she knew he was in his own world right now.

"Sophie is bringing over some of her finished blocks later, so you will be able to see how my white pieces fit in."

"Hmm," he responded, his mind already on other things.

"What happened when you called Jackson?"

He briefly filled her in about his conversation with Jackson and his own reservations about whether he would actually show up.

"You think he might not come?" she asked, her eyes on the seam allowance she was in the process of gluing down.

"It's possible," he said.

"Hmm," she responded, already lost in her own project.

Charles poured himself a cup of coffee, reluctantly took two healthy cookies from his cookie jar, and headed for the computer room.

Sarah sighed, realizing that their minds were on very different things right now. She felt somewhat distant from her husband when this happened, but she realized it was a good thing. The very fact that they both had interests they pursued on their own gave their lives together more depth, and when they met in the middle, they had much to share with each other.

About that time, Sophie burst in the door. She again came in through the garage, knowing that Sarah was working in the kitchen. "Look at these blocks that I made last night with the fabric we picked out at Stitches." She pulled out several of each fabric, bright oranges and yellows. "This gets much more sparkle in the quilt," she said, quoting a phrase she had heard Sarah use often over the years and now understood.

"You're having fun, aren't you?"

"You bet I am. I should have started doing this years ago."

Sarah just smiled, thinking about all the times she had encouraged her friend to try quilting, but she had always been met with objections. "I'm glad you're enjoying it," she said, raising an eyebrow.

"I know. I know. I should have listened to you."

"Pull up a chair, and let's see how my white paths look next to your blocks."

Sophie spread out several of her rosettes, and they placed the white hexagon path around them. "They are perfect!" Sophie exclaimed. "You keep making these segments, and

I'll start whipstitching them to my rosette blocks. We just might get this finished in time," she added, looking delighted.

"Are you going to make a label?" Sarah asked.

"Already done," Sophie responded, digging deep into her tote bag. She pulled out the label, and Sarah saw that Sophie had included her name as well.

"Oh, Sophie, this is your gift. I'm just helping. You shouldn't have my name on it."

"Without your influence and now your help, this would never have happened. Your name goes right there with mine."

Chapter 23

Lieutenant Matt Stokely took a seat on the sidelines and motioned for Charles to conduct the interview. Charles started by introducing Matt. Again, he explained that the department was looking at cold cases, in particular the death of his stepmother, Clarissa Davis.

"My father didn't kill her if that's what you're after. Doesn't your file say it was an accidental overdose?" Jackson appeared to be calm, but Charles could always sense when anger was smoldering just under the surface.

"Yes, and your father was cleared at the time, but we wanted to ask you a few questions if you're willing to talk to us. You aren't obligated to, but we'd appreciate it."

"Go ahead," Jackson said, slumping almost imperceptibly. "There's not much I can tell you at this point. That was more than thirty years ago. I was a thirteen-year-old kid."

Charles thanked Jackson and asked him to tell them about the night Clarissa died. Charles had read the reports and knew that Jackson had reported discovering his stepmother near death and had called 911. By the time the respondents arrived, Clarissa was pronounced dead. According to the investigating officer, the boy had been near hysterical and was taken into an emergency foster care placement since the father couldn't be located and there was no known family.

"I'm sorry she had to die, but I know it's the best thing that could have happened to our family."

Out of the side of his eye, Charles saw Stokely stiffen.

"Why do you say that, son?" Charles asked gently.

"Everything changed that day. They took me to this shelter for the night, but the next day Dad came and got me. We went to the police station so he could identify the body and he was trembling, but he was sober. I don't think he took another drink after that day. He said it was his fault and that he drove her to it."

"How so?"

"I guess he meant by the way he treated her. He beat her mercilessly. He would always say that she had asked for it, but I was afraid he'd kill her. Not on purpose, of course," Jackson added quickly, looking around at Stokely and back at Charles. "I just mean he was a big guy in those days, and Clarissa was just a tiny little thing. But something happened the day he went in to identify the body. It was like he started coming out of a fog that he'd been in for years. He stopped drinking and started going to Alcoholics Anonymous every day." Jackson stopped talking and seemed to be reliving those days in his mind.

Charles encouraged him to continue. "Go on, son," he said gently.

"A few days after the funeral, Dad said to me that this was no life for the boys. They'd been through too much he said, and he took them to Clarissa's mother and left them."

"Did he ever go back to see them?"

"I don't know. He said he never would. He said they were better off with him out of their lives. He thought there was still hope for them. He'd been beating those kids since they were toddlers. I heard they're both in prison now—is that true?" he asked, looking at Charles.

"That's true. What about you? Your dad left town right after that."

"Yeah, after the kids were gone and the investigation was over. Until then, we stayed in a motel in town. He didn't want to go back in the house. But he didn't drink, even then."

"Did you go with him when he left town?" Charles asked.

"Sure. He took me along. We drove south. I asked him where we were going, and he said he didn't know."

"Were you worried?"

"Not much. He wasn't drinking, and when we stopped for the night, he found a meeting, sometimes two. He started making more sense than he had in years, talking about getting a job in Louisiana and starting over."

"Why Louisiana?" Charles asked.

"He knew a guy down there. Turned out the guy was a preacher, which freaked me out."

"Why's that?"

"We'd never set foot in a church. But this guy, Pastor Tom, hugged my dad, and they cried together. I've got to say that really freaked me out. My dad crying? Anyway, we stayed with Pastor Tom and his family. We even started attending his church. Things were better for me and my dad."

"How long did you stay with Pastor Tom?"

"About three, maybe four months. I'm not sure. Dad got me into school, and we got an apartment in Tom's neighborhood. Dad got a job at this refrigeration place. I think Pastor Tom set it up. I saw Dad's boss in the congregation a few times. It was a trainee job and didn't pay much, but we got along okay. I was able to get odd jobs at a local store after school. He got promoted several times, and by the time I graduated, he was a technician and making decent money. He started looking at houses. Oh, I forgot to mention Angela."

"His second wife?"

"Yeah, he met her the year I graduated, and they got married a few years later. I don't know if she knew anything about his past. He was a different guy by then. Anyway, I went off to school in Texas and didn't get back home much. I don't know; I just sort of wanted him to have this new life without reminders of the past. We sent texts and called, and they drove down to Texas a couple of times to see me. I'm just so proud of my dad."

"And this is what you meant when you said Clarissa's death was the best thing that ever happened to your family?"

"You bet."

Charles avoided Stokely's eyes, thinking that they were probably both wondering the same thing. *Did Jackson kill his stepmother?* Charles' gut feeling was that he had not, but he knew not to trust those feelings completely.

"Would you like anything before we go on?" Charles asked. "Coffee? A coke?"

"Something cold would be good. Thanks." Charles started to stand, but Stokely was already up and said he'd take care of it.

Once Stokely returned with their drinks, Charles said, "Tell me about the day she died."

Jackson sighed deeply, rubbing his forehead. "It's hard to go there."

"I know, son. Just do the best you can. Tell us what you remember."

"First of all, you didn't know Clarissa. She was a doper, and I mean the hard stuff. Her body was covered with needle tracks. And she was always drunk or passed out. She didn't take care of the boys."

"Who did?"

"I did mostly."

Jackson again sat quietly, appearing to be debating whether to tell them something.

"Go on, son. It's been over thirty years. You don't have to keep her secrets any longer."

"She fooled around on dad all the time."

"Did he know it?"

"I guess so. Yeah," he added, dropping his eyes. "That's what most of the fights were about. But toward the end, there was this one guy that she was sweet on. I would see them together out back sometimes, and she seemed almost happy. He could make her laugh. It was the only time she laughed, just when she was with him."

"Do you know his name?" Stokely asked.

"Doug something. I don't guess I ever heard his last name. If I did, I don't remember it. She talked about him to me, but I never spent any time around him. They always left the house."

"How long did this continue?" Charles asked.

"About six months, I guess. Maybe more. She told me she was going away with him someday, and she asked me to look out for the boys once she was gone. She went on about that for a long time, and I was really hoping she would leave. I thought things would be better."

"Was she still seeing this guy up until she died?"

"Yes."

"Let's go back to that day. What's the first thing you remember about the day she died?"

"That afternoon when I came home, she was throwing stuff in a bag. She was very high on drugs and excited. She kept saying, 'This is it. He's coming for me tonight.' Anyway, she dragged her bag out by the old barn and sat out there until long after midnight."

"Where was your dad?" Charles asked.

"Dad never got home before 2:00 or 3:00, when the bars closed. Sometimes he never showed up at all. Anyway, every time I looked out back, she was sitting, waiting. The guy never came. Finally, I went out and told her I'd help her get her stuff back in the house. She'd been drinking and drugging out there. I didn't realize it until I went out.

"She couldn't even walk in. She was groggy and disoriented and said she was sick. I helped her into the bathroom and closed the door. She was wailing and out of her head. I was afraid Dad would get home. I put her suitcase under the bed so he wouldn't see it and went in to make coffee for her—not that it would have helped any. I don't know what she was taking, but I heard all this retching and then it got quiet.

"I knocked but she didn't answer, so I opened the door. She was laying on the floor unconscious. I figured she'd sleep it off, but something made me check her pulse, and it was very slow. I called for an ambulance, but she was dead by the time they arrived." Tears were running down his cheeks, but he seemed unaware and made no attempt to wipe them away.

"Do you think she took her life intentionally?"

"They said it was an accidental overdose. I'll never know. I think she was just finished."

"Finished?"

"Yeah. That's the only word I can think of to describe it. I think she'd just had all she could take of life. She was just through. Finished."

Charles remained quiet, allowing time for Jackson to process his feelings. Finally, Jackson wiped his face on his shirt sleeve and without looking up, said, "Bad as it was, she was the closest thing to a mother I ever had. I loved her. Underneath she was a good person. It was just the drugs and the beatings, and the hopelessness."

The three men continued to sit quietly for a while. Finally, Charles stood and thanked Jackson for coming in. "I know this has been hard for you, and we appreciate your willingness to share this with us."

"Yes," Stokely added. "Thank you for coming in."

The men shook hands, and Charles walked Jackson out of the room. "By the way, how's your father doing?" Charles asked as they were walking. "I know he must have been devastated by his second wife's death."

"He was, but I'm so proud of my dad. He hasn't touched a drop now in over thirty years. He's a deacon in Pastor Tom's church. I went to stay with him through the funeral and stayed on for a couple of months. Then he had that hearing to go through, even though there was no reason to suspect him. She died in a car accident, and he wasn't even with her. He loved her more than life."

"Again, thank you for coming in," Charles said when they reached the lobby.

Charles walked back to the interrogation room and found Stokely still sitting there.

"So?" Charles asked.

"My gut tells me that man had nothing to do with his stepmother's death."

"My gut agrees, and I also think the investigating officer back then got it right. It was probably accidental, but I doubt that the woman cared one way or the other whether she lived through it."

"Let's file this away," Matt said as he stood. "But thank you for pushing the department to take a second look. Sometimes it's good for all of us to be reminded that there are far more victims involved than just the one that's dead."

"And that the repercussions can go decades into the future," Charles responded.

* * * * *

"So what are we going to tell Maud?" Sarah asked once Charles filled her in on the details of the interview.

"I don't know. She's not going to believe what Jackson told us," Charles replied.

"I know," Sarah responded, looking downhearted. "She's held onto her fantasies about Clarissa for all these years, never admitting who she really was, not even to herself."

"Perhaps we should just let it drop. There's certainly nothing to tell her that will make her feel any better. Let's thank her for all her help, and hope that she can move on to a better place."

"I agree." Sarah reached down and scratched Barney's ears. He had been leaning against her leg, realizing that his person was distressed. "So, has Jamal been cleared?"

"Yes. They found several people willing to waive their anonymity and verify that Jamal was at an Alcoholics Anonymous meeting at the time of Angela's accident. As it turned out, they had nothing to go on anyway. It turned out there was a mechanical reason for the brakes to fail. That entire investigation was a waste of time."

"But our trip wasn't a waste of time," Sarah said, smiling. "It was a terrific use of time."

"You bet it was!"

"Let's go to that Louisiana restaurant they just opened in Hamilton and celebrate."

"Isn't that a long way to go for dinner?"

"Yes, but I need catfish," he responded with a silly grin.

Chapter 24

"I can make this real easy for you, Sarah," Norman said as he walked around the yard, snapping a twig here and there. "You have an excellent base. You have roses climbing up the fence, giving you a glorious backdrop, and they'll still be in bloom in early September. I'd suggest that you mulch the garden along the fence just to give it a nice fresh look, and then I recommend that you simply add pots of flowers here and there."

"What kind of flowers?"

"Whatever you like. Hydrangeas would look nice, and they come in soft colors, like pink, blue, and even white. Even pots of colorful asters would be very striking. Or lilies perhaps? Just whatever you like."

"Should I be potting the plants now?" Sarah asked, dreading the amount of work Norman was suggesting.

"No, no. Absolutely not! Go to the nursery and have them make the pots up for you." He reached into his pocket and pulled out a pile of business cards, which he thumbed through quickly, handing Sarah one. "These folks will put them together for you and deliver them just before the wedding. It'll cost you a few bucks, but it's much less stressful than planting now and hoping for results later. And they can also provide flowers for your tables. Are you serving a meal?"

"I'm not sure what she wants to do, so I think I'll just limit my involvement to the garden. She mentioned a simple garden party, but that's all up to her." Norman reached into his pocket and handed her a caterer's card.

"Tell Martha to call me if she has any questions or needs any help, gratis of course," he said as he handed her his own card as well. "We're practically family, you know."

Sarah, now with a handful of business cards, jerked her head up at his words. *Practically family? What did he mean by that? I have to get Sophie talking!* She tried to catch her friend's attention, but Sophie was clearly avoiding eye contact. As they were preparing to leave, Sarah said, "By the way, Sophie, tonight is quilt club, and I was hoping you'd pick me up. Charles said my car needs some work." She was intent on getting her friend alone, and in the car she'd have a captive audience.

"Sure," Sophie responded. "I'll come by for you at the usual time. Do you know what we're doing tonight?"

"Nothing special. I got an email this morning saying we should bring UFOs to work on."

"UFOs?" Norman repeated as both eyebrows jumped up his forehead.

Sophie chuckled, and Sarah responded, saying, "It stands for 'unfinished objects.' It refers to those projects we've all started and never finished."

"Why wouldn't a quilter want to finish her project?" Norman asked, unable to conceive of a project he might start and then not finish.

"Well, sometimes we run out of the right fabric for the project, and sometimes we just lose interest. I started a simple wallhanging two years ago, but I ended up packing it away."

"I remember that project," Sophie added, "and you stopped because you said there was a mistake in it, and I offered to take it apart for you."

"Does that offer still go?" Sarah asked, "Because if it does, I'll bring it tonight along with my new seam ripper."

"It's a deal," Sophie responded. "And I'll bring a pile of garden path hexagons for you to whipstitch together for me. I'm hoping to put a large section of the quilt together when you come over tomorrow."

"See you tonight," Sarah said as she waved to her friend and her curious cohort.

* * * * *

As they pulled up in front of Stitches, Sarah reached across Sophie and locked the door. "Okay, you are now my prisoner until you give me the straight scoop."

"Scoop? Scoop about what?" Sophie asked, looking wide-eyed and innocent.

"You know what I'm talking about. Here you are, dating a man that you've been very vague about, and now he refers to himself as 'practically family.' What's going on and why are you being so secretive?"

Sophie sat without speaking but had a look on her face that Sarah couldn't interpret. She looked anxious and distraught. "Are you okay, Sophie?"

"I'm okay, Sarah," Sophie responded, taking a deep breath. "I'm just so embarrassed about what happened last year with Higgy, and I was hoping to keep this whole thing under wraps until I learned more about this man. I figured with him being a wedding planner and our kids getting married, he could just be around without anyone realizing we were dating. I just don't trust my judgment anymore after that fiasco with Higginbottom."

The previous year, Sophie had become involved with a self-professed author who turned out to be simply an unsuccessful writer of atrocious greeting cards. She hadn't objected to that aspect of the relationship but ended up being devastated when he turned out to be married to a Las Vegas showgirl with whom he ultimately reunited, leaving Sophie with a broken heart and feeling humiliated.

"Sophie, do I have to remind you what friends are for? You need to trust me. I love you no matter what, and I want to be there for you whenever you are hurt or scared or happy or whatever you might be feeling, just like you are for me. Now," she added, with a mischievous grin, "let's get down to the nitty-gritty here. How do you feel about this man?"

"I love the attention. And he makes me laugh."

"Two great things!" Sarah replied. "And?"

"And he really seems to care about me. He's interested in my quilting and my family. He wants to get to know my friends. So far, so good," she added with a slight blush. Sarah decided not to push it any farther. She also wanted to give her friend the privacy she needed to explore this new relationship and her own feelings.

"Thank you, Sophie. I was feeling very left out."

"Oh, I didn't mean to leave you out, Sarah. I'm sorry. I'm just new at all this, you know. I was married to Timmy's father for nearly fifty years, even though he didn't know me the last five of those years. Then there was the Higginbottom disaster. I'm just a little hesitant … and then there's this whole wedding planner thing."

"What wedding planner thing?"

"Well, don't you think it's a little odd for a man to be a wedding planner? My hairdresser was surprised when I told her I was seeing a wedding planner. She said most wedding planners are gay."

"Sophie, that's ridiculous. That's just some silly stereotype. He told us why he chose his career, and I think it said a great deal about him. He loves to make people happy and be with them on special occasions. He seems like a very extraordinary person and an artist of a sort."

"That's the way I feel about him, too, but I don't want to rush into anything. I must admit that I've been very happy with my life the past years, being free to do what I want, and I love the feeling of being independent and able to take care of myself. It's just that sometimes I see you and Charles together, and a part of me thinks it would be nice to be part of a couple. I just don't know …"

"Say no more, my friend. I totally understand. Take your time and keep doing exactly what you're doing. I just appreciate that you've told me what's going on. Now I won't be worried about you. Let get to those UFOs." They got out of the car and headed into the shop.

"Oh, I forgot to tell you! Paula wants us to come to her house tomorrow afternoon. She has some information for us."

Sophie squealed with excitement. "I'll bring my cards!"

Chapter 25

The next afternoon, Sarah and Sophie arrived at Paula's full of excitement. Paula was kneeling in her flower bed when they arrived, and she stood and waved. "Come on in," she called as she headed for the door. "I'm going to wash up, and I'll meet you two in the kitchen. There's iced tea in the fridge and glasses are chilling in the freezer. Help yourself to pastries."

"Take your time," Sarah called as she stopped to look at the begonias her friend was planting. "Sophie, we need to go to the nursery and begin making arrangements for the pots of flowers. I want the garden to look perfect for the wedding reception." Correcting herself, she said, "Actually Martha is calling it a garden party, and they've requested no gifts."

"Well, they can just forget that one. They are getting at least two gifts, our quilt and your honeymoon trip. Have you and Charles decided where to send them?"

"Charles is working on that one. He has found several excellent packages to the Caribbean. We talked about a cruise, but they don't want to be away very long. We're thinking four or five days in the islands, perhaps."

"Perfect!" Sophie replied.

By the time Paula came into the kitchen dressed in fresh shorts and a tee-shirt, Sarah had the tea poured. Paula had prepared the table ahead of time with dessert dishes, napkins, and a plate of assorted pastries covered in plastic wrap. Sophie had already helped herself to a pastry. "Hope you don't mind," she mumbled apologetically with a full mouth. Paula gave her a thumbs up and grabbed one for herself before she sat down.

After the three had socialized for a few minutes, Paula reached for her legal pad, saying, "I know you're eager to see what I've found. I hope you aren't going to be disappointed."

Paula glanced at her notes and then looked up at the two women. She said, "If Agatha referred to the quilt as a family heirloom, it's most likely an heirloom from her side of the family. Agatha's husband, John Tarkington, immigrated to this country from England. He was listed as traveling alone in the 1920s, and I think it's unlikely that the quilt came from his side of the family."

"I agree, and we neglected to mention that Harry Wilkinson, the man who told us about Agatha in the first place, thought that she had inherited it from her mother. Did you find anything about Agatha's side of the family?"

"I did. I was able to find Agatha's parents, Elizabeth Bell and George Hayes. They were married in 1901 and had one child, Agatha, who was born the next year and died in 1965. By the way, I confirmed that Agatha had no children or siblings. She married John Tarkington when she was twenty, and they were divorced a few years later."

"Harry told us she died of cancer in her sixties."

"She did. So then I went back a generation and looked into Agatha's grandparents. Her grandmother was Annie Dean, born in 1850. Annie married a William Bell in 1870, and they had three babies right away, all stillborn. Then Elizabeth, Agatha's mother, was born in 1877."

"None of this tells us anything about who made the quilt," Sophie interjected, sounding discouraged.

"Well, we're getting there … not necessarily to the quilt, but I was able to go back one more step, and I found one interesting thing that might help you."

"What's that?"

"Annie's parents, Agatha's great-grandparents, were Madeline Rainey and John Dean. They were both born in 1820, married in 1842, and had four children. The oldest were twin boys, Nathan and Matthew, born in 1844. Then there was Annie, who was born in 1850, and there was a baby boy, Nicholas, who died at age two."

"So this gets us back to just prior to the Civil War, but what about the quilt?" Sophie asked again. "I don't see how this helps."

"None of this directly helps, but let me tell you the one thing I found of interest in the 1850's census. The Dean household, which by then included Madeline and John, the twin boys, and baby girl Annie, also included a twenty-two-year-old woman named Mabel who was listed as Madeline's sister. It wasn't uncommon for unmarried women to be living either with their parents or their siblings at that time. Also, Madeline died young, and Mabel may have been helping with the children."

"And how does this help us?" Sophie asked but then noticed that Sarah seemed to have caught on.

"So there may be another line of family members we could be considering," Sarah announced, "assuming this Mabel married at some point."

"That's exactly it. I started going in the other direction and tracked Mabel back down the line and found that she has a great-great-great-granddaughter living right here in Middletown."

"If Agatha had family here in town, wouldn't she have known about her?" Sophie asked.

"Maybe, maybe not," Paula responded. "Strange things happen within families. They were a small family and may have never known about one another. Agatha would have been much younger. At any rate, I have her name and address for you if you'd like to contact her. There's always the chance that she knows something about the family. She would be a distant cousin of Agatha Tarkington, but she's in her nineties and apparently, from what you've told me, never met Agatha."

"It sounds pretty unlikely that she'll have any information about an obscure cousin's family history, but it's worth a try," Sarah responded with a hint of disappointment.

Paula wrote out the contact information for her friend and said she hoped it would lead to something. "I know how badly you want to find out about your quilt, but this is the kind of information that gets lost over time. We're talking about more than 150 years."

Sarah thanked Paula profusely for all her help and Sophie gathered up her 3″ by 5″ cards that she had brought in order to record all the new information.

"What next?" Sophie asked as they were getting into the car. She pulled the 3″ by 5″ card out of her bundle where she had transcribed the woman's name and address.

"Virginia Binning," she read. "1300 Oakmont Drive. Isn't that just on the other side of Ruth's quilt shop? Like three or four streets toward town?"

"I think you're right. I don't want to just stop by, but let's drive by there on our way home. I need some batting for my hexagon table topper, so we can stop by Running Stitches while we're over there."

The house was a small white frame with a large maple tree in the front yard. There was neatly trimmed ivy planted under the tree and a garden bench beneath the far-reaching limbs. The front porch extended the width of the house and was decorated with potted coleus and geraniums. A petite, gray-haired woman was sitting in the porch swing, apparently concentrating on some sort of handwork.

"Should we stop?" Sophie asked.

"I don't feel comfortable just stopping by, Sophie. I don't want to catch the woman totally off guard. I'll call her later this afternoon and perhaps we can see her tomorrow." She turned around at the next intersection and drove up the street to the fabric shop.

"Virginia Binning? Of course I know Virginia," Ruth responded with a warm smile. "She's been a customer of mine for years, in fact, as long as I've been open. She was one of my first customers. Why do you ask?"

"Her name has come up in my search for the history of the *Memories* quilt." Sarah decided not to share any more of the story until she spoke with Virginia personally. "She's a quilter?"

"She sure is. She pieces and quilts by hand and does gorgeous work. When I first opened, she did classes for me in hand piecing, but over time there seemed to be less and less demand. Everyone wanted to work by machine so they could get things made quickly. Virginia always wanted to take her time and quilt the way her family had before her."

Sarah's ears perked up at that, hoping that this woman was going to have some information for her. She headed home to make the call.

Chapter 26

"Why sure," the woman responded enthusiastically after Sarah explained that she was trying to track down the history of an old quilt. She hadn't gone into the family connections, saving that for when they got together. "I'd be happy to have you and your friend come by."

"When would be a good time?" Sarah asked.

"Tomorrow afternoon would work best for me. I have a few doctor appointments this week, but I'm free tomorrow. Could you come around 3:00 in the afternoon? I try to take a short nap after lunch."

"That sounds fine. We'll bring the quilt and see you then."

"Now, I don't want to get your hopes up," Virginia added. "I don't know much about vintage quilts, although I have a few here you might like to see. I'll get them out before you come."

* * * * *

The next afternoon, Sarah arrived alone. Sophie had made plans with Norman that she offered to cancel, but Sarah encouraged her to go on out with Norman, and she'd fill Sophie in on everything she learned. "I don't expect much," Sarah had said, knowing it was unlikely this distant relative would know anything about the quilt.

Virginia had iced tea ready when Sarah arrived, and she apologized about the lack of air conditioning. "This old house usually stays pretty cool, but it's unusually hot this week." They chatted for a while, mostly about quilting and about Virginia's long relationship with Ruth and Running Stitches. Finally Virginia said, "Let's see that quilt of yours."

When Sarah pulled the quilt out of the bag, Virginia gasped, placing her hand over her heart as the color drained from her face.

"Are you okay?" Sarah exclaimed, hurrying to her side. "Should I call someone?"

"No, I'm okay. It was just a shock to see that quilt."

"Why is that?" Sarah asked, leading Virginia to the couch. She placed a pillow behind Virginia and reached for her glass of tea.

"Hand me that box please," Virginia said once she caught her breath. "I have something to show you."

"Are you sure you can handle this?" Sarah asked, still very concerned about the frail woman.

"Yes, I'll be fine. You'll understand in a minute."

Sarah placed the box on the couch next to Virginia, wiping away some of the dust with her hand.

"Sorry. It's been in the attic for years," Virginia explained. "I went up for it last night. I couldn't believe the number of old things up there I should have gotten rid of years ago …" But she stopped talking and turned her attention to the box. She removed the string which held it closed. "After my mother died, I found this box in the back of her closet.

It was dust covered, as if it had been there for many years. Apparently, it had been passed down to her as well."

She reached in and pulled out a small appliquéd quilt which she laid aside. "My mother made this one. I added it to this box after mother died."

"But this," she said before pulling out the second quilt, "was made by my great-great-great-aunt, Madeline Rainey."

It was Sarah's turn to gasp and grab her heart. "*Memories*!" she exclaimed. "It's the other half of *Memories*!" Sarah sank into a nearby chair. "I don't understand. Where did you get this?"

"It was passed down in my family. I wouldn't know anything about it if it weren't for the Bible that was in the box along with the quilt."

"The Bible?" Sarah repeated with astonishment.

Virginia reached into the box and pulled out a very old and ragged Bible held together by a black silk ribbon. She carefully opened the Bible in the middle and handed it to Sarah. Sarah read through the carefully written names and dates, going back to the early 1800s. She recognized some of the names as being ones Paula had found along with the dates of their births, marriages, and deaths. She saw little Nicholas' name, Annie, and the twin boys, as well as Madeline's sister, Mabel.

A list of other relatives followed that Sarah didn't recognize, most likely those in Mabel's branch of the family, leading to Virginia. "Mabel was my great-great-great-grandmother," Virginia said proudly, pointing to her mother's name. Moving her finger down a line, she pointed to Madeline's name. "And Madeline was her sister. Madeline made the quilt."

"How do you know that?" Sarah gasped.

"By reading this," Virginia responded, handing Sarah an old discolored envelope that was tucked in the back of the Bible. Sarah was afraid to open it for fear it would crumble in her hand. "It's okay," Virginia said. "Just open it carefully. I've only taken it out once." Sarah carefully removed the several sheets of paper, obviously a letter written many years ago.

"I taped the creases from the back. I probably shouldn't have, but it seemed important to keep it from tearing," Virginia said. "Take it out on the porch and read it. It needs to be read privately."

Sarah sat down in the swing where she had first seen Virginia sitting. She slipped on her reading glasses and began reading.

I'll be gone before spring arrives. I told them to put my grave next to Nicholas' on the knoll behind grandpa's farm. I'll be the fourth to be buried in the family graveyard. Uncle John was first, then Mama, and finally my little Nicholas. The knoll has been cleared and planted with bulbs and wildflowers. It's a mass of color in the summer, but in the winter it's barren and cold.

My family and friends will meet at the chapel for a solemn service. I wish they'd make it festive. My life has been shortened, but the Lord has been good to me, and I want the family to celebrate that.

Last night I heard my sister, Mabel, whispering in the hall. She wants to bury me with my Memories *quilt, but I promised it to young Annie. I called out to Mabel, and she tiptoed into my room, whispering as if the sound of her voice might cause my death. I told her that Annie was to have the quilt.*

Mama and I started Memories *together in the fall of 1854 when Annie was only four. Annie made a few stitches that year and many more in years to come. The fabrics are from my dear children's clothes and scraps from Mama's basket. Mabel spent hours working with me at the quilting frame after Mama was gone.*

Everyone in the family has a place in that quilt. They would sit around the fire at night while I was working at the frame and the children would squeal, "Look, that's from my old dress," or "Remember when Papa wore that shirt?" Annie could point to any piece and say who it had belonged to, even though many of the people were long gone by then.

She has a memory for things family. Annie promised me that she will keep the quilt in the family where it belongs for years to come.

I had to set Memories aside when Nicholas was born. What with his sickness, my own weakness, and caring for the house and the other children, there was no time left for frivolous sewing. Not that year, nor the next for that matter. I often took the unfinished quilt out of the cedar chest and held it to my heart. Mama was gone by that time, but I could still see her in her tiny stitches. I finished it this winter—just in time.

Yes, I'm glad Annie will have the quilt. She'll keep it in the family.

Madeline Rainey

February 2, 1859

A note had been added at the bottom of the last page in a different handwriting dated October 4, 1861, and signed by Madeline's sister, Mabel Rainey.

> *Today Madeline's twin boys left to join the soldiers. Annie and I cut the* Memories *quilt down the middle and quickly added a binding to the cut edges so that each boy would have half of his mother's quilt to remind them of their mother's love. She died so young, leaving young Annie and the boys. Annie had promised to treasure the quilt, but she knew her mother would want Nathan and Matthew to have it with them to remind them of her love. We both cried as we cut the quilt and again as we watched the boys trudging down the dusty road with their meager possessions strapped to their backs.*

Sarah sat feeling numb. Finally she stood and returned to the living room, where she found Virginia with tears running down her cheeks. "It's a sad story," Virginia muttered. "I'm sorry to have to share it with you."

"I'm glad you did. I've needed to know."

They sat quietly for a while when Sarah suddenly looked up and said, "But both halves of the quilt made it back. That means the boys came home."

"No, my mother knew that part of the story. Only Nathan came home, carrying both quilts. He was with his brother when he died, but he had been buried by the time his quilt was located. Nathan brought it home with him, but he died shortly after from his own injuries."

"And they gave both halves to Annie?"

"No one knows how that was decided, but each half ended up being passed down the two lines: Madeline's line and Mabel's."

"That seems only fair since they made it together."

"Now what?" Sarah asked, knowing that she should offer her half to Virginia.

"I think we should take them into Hamilton to the quilt museum and tell them everything we know," Virginia announced.

"Oh, Virginia, I think that's exactly what we should do. How would you feel about giving them the letter, too?"

"I have no living children, Sarah. I'd be willing to donate the Bible as well. This is history that deserves to be shared."

Virginia stood and wrapped her arms around her new friend as they grieved for people long gone.

Chapter 27

Six weeks later …

Sarah and Sophie were sitting in two of the dozen or so cushioned wicker chairs the caterer had arranged strategically in Sarah and Charles' backyard. "The garden looks beautiful," Sophie commented as she sipped her frothy island drink.

"You can take that umbrella out of your drink," Sarah said, noticing that her friend was having trouble drinking around it.

Several people were arriving, and Sarah stood to greet them. She didn't recognize any of the women but thought she had seen one of the men in Martha's office. He approached Sarah smiling and introduced himself and his wife and the other two couples. "We're the lab contingency." An attractive young woman who was with them held out her hand and said, "And I'm Sylvia. I think we met when you stopped by the lab last month."

"Yes, Sylvia. I'm so glad you came."

"We met a few men outside the chapel that introduced themselves as Timothy's coworkers from the firehouse,"

Sylvia said. "They asked me to tell you that they were on their way. They needed to stop by the station first."

"So glad to meet all of you," Sarah said. "They've set up a bar just over there," she added, pointing to a man in a white jacket who was arranging glasses on the patio. "Get a drink and find a comfortable spot to relax. Martha said she and Tim would be along soon. They're having a few pictures taken at the chapel."

"It was a lovely ceremony," one of the wives said. "Thank you for including us. Martha said it was going to be primarily family, and we were honored to be included."

"They both wanted a few special friends," Sarah responded with a welcoming smile. "Come meet Timothy's mother and daughter," she added, motioning for the group to follow her. Penny had joined her grandmother and was sipping a matching frothy drink with an umbrella, but without the alcohol.

"Hey, Sophie," a young man hollered from the gate.

"Those are the firemen we met earlier," Sylvia said, fluffing her hair and smiling in their direction.

Sarah introduced the people from the lab and was surprised to see the firemen crowding around Sophie, talking excitedly.

Turning to Sarah, Sophie said, "Have you met this rowdy bunch?" She introduced them by name, to Sarah's surprise. Sarah later learned that Tim had taken her to the station to see where he worked, and she had entertained them with her repertoire of greatly embellished stories about life in their retirement community.

There were now a dozen people crowded around Sophie, which of course put her in performance mode, and within minutes she had them all howling with laughter. It was Sophie's unique talent. She could find the hilarious side of anything, and in this case, she was describing how today's party had grown from a casual wine and cheese get-together to a full-blown catered luncheon.

Sarah's son, Jason, and his wife arrived a few minutes later, having taken the children to their other grandmother for the afternoon. Andy and Caitlyn came through the gate next, and Penny ran to meet them, leaving Sarah and Sophie alone again.

"I could handle another one of these drinks," Sophie announced as she held her empty glass in the air. The attentive bartender signaled and immediately appeared with two umbrella drinks, handing one to Sarah. "Your son said to bring you this."

Sarah thanked him and put it on the wicker table between her and Sophie. "It's perfect weather," she commented, looking up at the fluffy white clouds gently floating across a cerulean sky.

"It's been a perfect day in every way," Sophie replied. "I wish there had been more people in the chapel to enjoy the beauty of it all. Your daughter was stunning, and my son was rather striking himself."

"He sure was, Sophie. He looked very dignified in that suit. But remember, a small ceremony with just their closest friends and family was what they both wanted."

"True, but they also wanted an informal get-together in your backyard, and I believe I see a linen tablecloth and napkins, not to mention a handsome bartender and waitstaff running back and forth."

"And who's responsible for that?" Sarah asked with a playful grin.

"Okay, I'll admit there was a bit of devious meddling going on, but neither one seemed to mind."

At that moment the back gate opened, and everyone stood and began clapping and cheering. "That must be our kids," Sophie said, wiggling out of her chair to stand. The clapping continued as the newly married couple walked across the yard, hugging friends as they headed for their extremely proud mothers.

"Where's Charles?" Martha asked, looking around.

"He and Norman had something to take care of," Sarah responded. "They'll be right back." Martha gave her a quizzical look but shrugged and noticed Andy nearby. Tim had already spotted him and guided her over to where Andy was standing. "Congratulations, old man," Sarah heard him say as the men were shaking hands. She saw her daughter kiss Andy's cheek and heard her giggle as he whispered something in her ear. Sarah knew for sure this was the happiest day in her daughter's life.

Not long after Charles and Norman returned, the caterer requested that the guests be seated for lunch. There were two long tables placed together to form a table long enough to seat all the guests. The table was covered with a white linen tablecloth, and simple centerpieces of red roses and baby's breath were placed along the middle of the table every few feet. Martha had rejected the idea of place cards and encouraged everyone to choose their seat, but she had already picked places for herself and Tim on one side near the middle of the table. She said, "You four sit across from us," looking at Sarah and Sophie.

"The four of us?" Sophie responded, looking confused.

"The mothers, Charles, and Norman," Martha replied in a matter-of-fact tone.

"Norman?" Sophie responded.

"Of course," Martha replied just as Norman walked up behind Sophie. "Without that man we'd be sitting on metal folding chairs and eating cheese and stale crackers."

"Now, Martha," Norman responded in a diminutive tone. "You did it all."

"With your help, Norman, and your sense of style. You made it perfect, and I can never thank you enough."

Most of Martha's coworkers found seats on Martha's side of the table except for the single young woman, Sylvia, who found a seat in the midst of the firemen and was enjoying their raucous attention.

Sarah looked around for Penny and found her at the far end of the table. "Why isn't Penny up here with us?"

Martha responded, "She wanted to sit with Caitlyn and Andy. Besides, she's taken a liking to Scott, the young fireman sitting next to her."

"She's too young to be taking a liking to anyone," Sophie grumbled, but she got over it immediately when Martha asked Charles and Norman where they had gone.

"We went to pick up dessert," Charles responded.

"Dessert?" Martha repeated, looking confused. "We have a wedding cake for dessert."

"Not that kind of dessert," Charles responded.

Martha looked at him curiously but ultimately shrugged and picked up her fork.

The caterer had served the first course, consisting of a thick slice of red tomato and an equally thick slice of mozzarella with basil olive oil drizzled over the top.

Two young men serving as waitstaff filled their wine glasses in preparation for the toasts.

Later when the main course arrived, Martha smiled with pleasure and sent Norman an appreciative look. The elegant plate featured a large split puff pastry filled with flaky salmon in a cream sauce and accompanied by dark green asparagus and a rice dish with almonds and dried cranberries.

Everyone lingered over their meal, clearly enjoying a pleasant afternoon. After the dishes had been taken away, a simple wedding cake was brought out and placed in front of the wedding couple for Martha to cut. She sliced a piece and fed it to her new husband while everyone cheered and applauded. "I wonder what your elderly neighbors are thinking about all this?" one of the firemen said to Sarah.

The caterer returned and took the cake into the kitchen, quickly returning with her staff carrying trays with slices of cake for everyone and several pots of coffee. The bartender followed with a bottle of Kahlúa for anyone who wanted their coffee spiked.

Relaxed and well fed, the group remained sitting around the table long after all evidence of the meal had been removed. They laughed, told embarrassing tales on both Timothy and Martha, and generally just had a great time. Sarah noticed that Sophie and Norman were holding hands.

At one point Charles stood and said, "Martha and Tim, I know you said that you didn't want gifts, but this isn't exactly a gift … it's more like a replacement …"

"What?" Martha said looking confused. "A replacement? Don't tell me you want to take away that gorgeous quilt Sophie made for us," she cried. "I'll never give it up!"

"No," Charles chuckled. "We aren't going to replace your quilt. What we have in mind replacing is your plan to drive out to the lake for a few days."

"With what?" she asked, tilting her head, not quite sure what was going on.

"With this," Charles said as he handed Martha a brochure describing a tropical beach resort in Bermuda. He then handed two tickets to Tim. "Your flight leaves at noon tomorrow, and Sarah and I will pick you up at 9:00, so don't stay up too late."

There was a bit of snickering at the firemen's end of the table.

Both Timothy and Martha were speechless. "But my work ..." Martha started to say.

"Covered," her boss called from the other end of the table.

"And I have ..." Tim started to say.

"Covered," came simultaneously from three of the firemen.

Timothy shook his head and appeared to be overwhelmed. He could only mutter, "This is too good to be true."

Martha began reading through the brochure. "Look, Tim—white beaches, a tropical island, snorkeling, and boating excursions. Oh and look! The resort has a spa, their own restaurant overlooking the ocean, island tours ... oh, Tim, look at the rooms!" She leaned over so he could see the brochure. He kissed her cheek and looked at her with such love Sarah thought she would weep. Sarah reached over and took her husband's hand, and they looked at each other, both knowing they couldn't have found a better gift.

"Oh," Martha said, suddenly remembering that she was now a parent. "What about Penny?"

"Covered!" Penny called from the other end of the table.

"What do you mean 'covered?' " her father asked in a firm parental tone.

"We've worked it out. I'm staying for three days with grandmother and three days with Caitlyn."

"You knew about this?" he asked, turning to Sophie.

"Sure did, and you thought I couldn't keep a secret."

"And you knew, too, pumpkin?" he called down to Penny.

"Yep."

"Wow. What a family," he responded, shaking his head. "Thank you, Sarah and Charles. This is way too much, but we appreciate it more than you can imagine. It's the perfect beginning to a perfect life."

Martha stood and walked around the table to hug her mother and Charles. "Thank you, Mom and Dad. I love you both."

As she walked away, Charles reached for Sarah's hand and smiled. "I finally have a daughter," he whispered.

"And a granddaughter!" Sarah replied just as Penny ran over to hug them both.

PROJECT

See full quilt on back cover.

TATTERED & TORN

Sophie made a replica of this scrappy vintage 74½″ × 82½″ Grandmother's Flower Garden as a wedding present. Make your quilt this size, or make a table topper with only nine rosettes, as done in Delores' English paper-piecing class.

MATERIALS

2½″-wide fabric strips to total:

- 4¼ yards for outer rings
- 2¼ yards for middle rings
- ½ yard for rosette centers
- 3 yards for garden path

Fusible wash-away foundation paper, such as Wash-Away Appliqué Sheets (by C&T Publishing): 114 sheets 8½″ × 11″ (5 packs if using Wash-Away Appliqué Sheets)

Backing: 5 yards

Batting: 83″ × 90″

Bias binding: ⅞ yard

Water-soluble glue stick

Project Instructions

MAKE THE ROSETTES

1. Print or trace the hexagon pattern (page 213) on the fusible foundation paper. Cut out the hexagon.
2. Following the package directions, fuse the foundation-paper hexagon to the wrong side of the fabric. Cut the fabric ¼″ outside of the fused hexagon for seam allowances.
3. Fold the seam allowances under at the edge of the foundation paper. Glue the seam allowance to the wrong side. Make as many hexagons as desired.
4. Whipstitch a middle-ring hexagon to a rosette-center hexagon, right sides together. Whipstitch 5 more middle-ring hexagons to the rosette center. Whipstitch the side of each hexagon to its neighbor as you add it to the center.

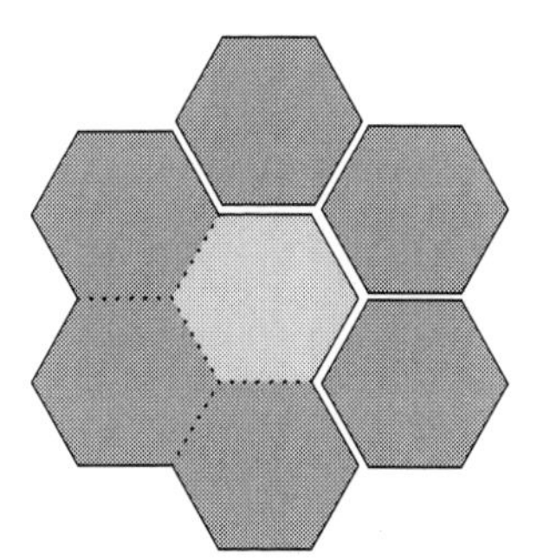

Beginning the rosette

5. When the middle ring is complete, add 12 outer-ring hexagons to complete the rosette.
6. Make 76 whole rosettes and 10 half-rosettes. (Half-rosettes have a center hexagon, 4 middle-ring hexagons, and 7 outer-ring hexagons.)

ASSEMBLE THE COLUMNS

1. **Column A:** Whipstitch 2 garden-path hexagons to the bottom of a half-rosette. Whipstitch a whole rosette to the bottom of the 2 garden-path hexagons. Continue adding garden-path hexagons and then rosettes for a total of 8 rosettes. Add 2 more garden-path hexagons and the final half-rosette. Make 5 of Column A.
2. **Column B:** Whipstitch 2 garden-path hexagons to the bottom of a rosette. Whipstitch another rosette to the bottom of the 2 garden-path hexagons. Continue adding garden-path hexagons and then rosettes for a total of

9 rosettes. Add 2 garden-path hexagons to the top and bottom of the column. Make 4 of Column B.

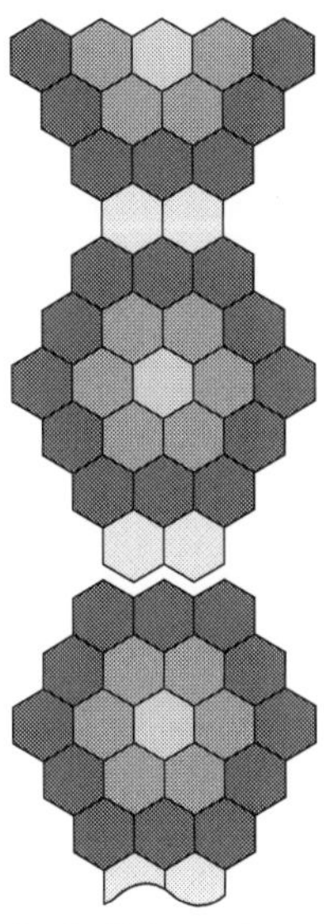

Begin Column A with a half-rosette.

ASSEMBLE AND FINISH THE QUILT

1. Whipstitch garden-path hexagons to the right edge of each column.

Add the garden path to each column.

2. Starting with a Column A, whipstitch the columns together, alternating A and B. There will be a garden path between the columns and at the right edge of the quilt.

3. Add garden-path hexagons to the left edge of the quilt.
4. Layer the pieced top with the batting and backing. Quilt and bind as desired.

> **Tip** || Use a bias binding to smoothly bind the jagged edges of this quilt.

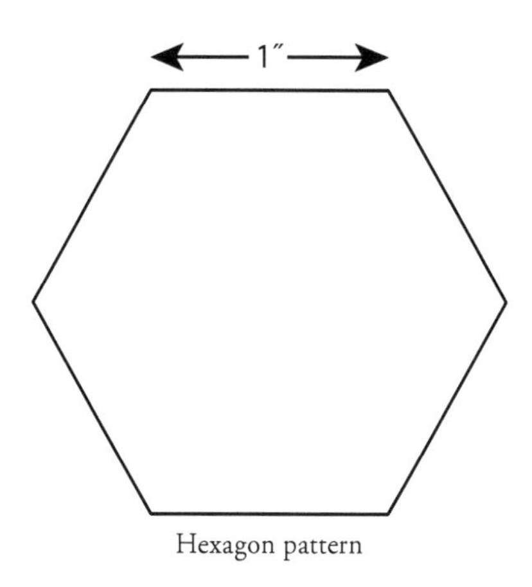

Hexagon pattern

Turn the page for a preview of the next book in A Quilting Cozy series.

PREVIEW

2nd edition includes instructions to make the featured quilt

Left Holding the Bag

a quilting cozy

Carol Dean Jones

Preview of *Left Holding the Bag*

"Some woman is moving into your house," Sophie announced excitedly when Sarah answered the phone.

"My house? What do you mean?"

"Your old house," Sophie explained. "There's a van out there, and I saw them carry in two sewing machines. Do you suppose she quilts?" Sophie added eagerly.

When Sarah first moved to the retirement community, she lived in a one-story townhome directly across the street from Sophie. Since that time, Sarah had married a retired detective and moved to a single-family home just a few blocks away and still within the community.

"She may be a quilter," Sarah responded. "I'm sure we'll find out soon. Let's give her time to get settled, and then perhaps we can stop by and welcome her."

"Great idea, and that's why I'm calling," Sophie responded. "I just made an apple pie, and I'm taking it over. Do you want to come with me?"

"Aren't the movers still there?" Sarah asked.

"Yes, but …"

"Sophie, slow down. Let the poor woman get moved in before descending on her." Sophie was always eager to get involved when new people moved into Cunningham Village and had been a godsend to Sarah when she arrived, alone and feeling desolate. After her husband had died and her daughter had convinced her to move into a retirement community, she had lost everything that was familiar to her. And that's when Sophie came knocking on her door. Remembering how much that visit had meant to her, Sarah began to back down. "Maybe we could just stop by for a minute and welcome her," she said hesitantly.

"That's exactly what I was thinking. Come on over, and we'll take the pie to her. And bring ice cream if you have any."

Sarah sighed and pulled a container of French vanilla ice cream from the freezer still holding the phone. She was glad to be getting rid of it since it had been a constant struggle to keep Charles on the diet his doctor had ordered after his most recent stroke.

"I'm on my way," Sarah replied, hanging up the phone and reaching for a jacket. It was mid-April, and there was a nip in the air earlier when she let Barney out.

Sarah felt somewhat better about descending upon the new neighbor once she turned the corner and saw that the moving van was pulling away. *At least she's alone now*, Sarah assured herself. *It won't seem quite so intrusive.*

Sophie was waiting on her porch when Sarah walked up with Barney in tow. "Your dog's coming with us?" Sophie commented in a disapproving tone.

"No, I thought Barney could stay in your backyard and play with Emma until we get back."

"Good idea," Sophie exclaimed. "Emma's been moping around here all morning waiting for Norman." Sophie's new gentleman friend had been dropping by most mornings for coffee and had been taking Emma to the dog park. "My hip's been acting up, and I haven't been walking her much. We just wait for Norman, but I haven't heard from him this morning," she added looking disappointed. "Maybe he's not coming today."

Sarah smiled to herself, thinking how good Norman has been for her friend. They got together almost daily and sent text messages back and forth when they were apart.

"Oh, there he is now," Sophie exclaimed, looking down at her phone which had just signaled an incoming text. "Oh," she said reading his message. "He's not coming until later, but he wants to take me to lunch. Wait a minute while I respond." She sat down and punched a few buttons, then slipped the phone back into her pocket and smiled impishly. "He'll be here in an hour."

When Sarah tapped on the door that used to be her own, it was opened by a tall, attractive woman who appeared to be somewhat younger than most of the village residents. "I'd say she's in her early sixties," Sarah was to tell her husband Charles later.

Sarah and Sophie introduced themselves, and Sophie handed the woman the tote bag which contained the pie and ice cream. She pointed out that the pie was hot and the ice cream cold and that the woman might want to separate them right away. Sarah knew Sophie was hoping for a serving of each, but their new neighbor took them into the kitchen and stuck them both in the refrigerator. Sophie started to suggest that she leave the pie out since it was warm, but Sarah poked her and shook her head.

"I'm Bernice Jenkins," the woman said, "and you'll have to excuse the mess …"

"We know what it's like to be moving," Sarah responded, hoping to put the woman at ease. "Is there anything we can do to help?" Sarah glanced around the room, looking for something familiar, but with the boxes and drop clothes, she didn't see anything of her old home.

Sophie was still waiting for an invitation to sit and have pie and ice cream, but the invitation never came. "I appreciate the thought. That was very kind of you both," the woman said as she walked back toward the front door. "I hope we can get together soon and get to know each other, but right now I've got to start dealing with these boxes. Again, thank you." By that time, she had the front door open, and there was no choice but for Sarah and Sophie to walk through it and cross the street to Sophie's house.

"That was strange," Sophie said once they were inside. Sarah went into Sophie's kitchen to let the dogs in and returned to the living room where Sophie was now sitting by the window.

"It was indeed strange," Sarah agreed, "but she just arrived and probably is overwhelmed by all the work ahead of her."

"I suppose you're right," Sophie responded, "but it felt like a major brush-off to me."

A few minutes later they heard a car pull up. Sophie peeked through the curtains and announced that a straggly looking young man was getting out of the car. "Now the car's pulling away and the guy just walked into Bernice's house without knocking."

"I'm sure it's okay, Sophie. Let's make a pot of tea."

"I don't know," Sophie replied shaking her head. "That rusted-out heap of a car and that ragtag guy—something just doesn't seem right."

Nothing else was said about the new neighbor until Sophie and Sarah sat down to tea. "I just hope that guy isn't over there eating my apple pie," Sophie grumbled.

* * * * *

"How old was the guy?" Charles asked after Sarah caught him up on her morning activities with Sophie.

"I didn't see him, but Sophie said he looked like he might be in his early twenties, but she said it was hard to tell. She said he looked unkempt, like some of the homeless men that come to the soup kitchen where she volunteers. But Bernice must have known him. He walked right in without knocking."

"She might have been expecting him, and that's why you and Sophie got the brush-off when you took Sophie's pie and my ice cream to her."

"First of all, it wasn't your ice cream. I bought that for the kids when they're here. Your lowfat, sugar-free ice cream is right there in the freezer, but you might be right about what felt like a brush-off. He arrived shortly after we left."

"How long did he stay?"

"We didn't see him leave, but we were in the kitchen. He might still be there for all I know."

At that moment, the phone rang.

"Hi, Sophie," Sarah answered. "I thought you were going out to lunch?"

"Norman and I just left, but I noticed that Bernice's car is gone now."

"She's probably gone to the store," Sarah responded.

"I could see her in the kitchen. She doesn't have her curtains up yet."

"And you think maybe the man that was there took her car?"

"I believe that's possible."

Sarah had the phone on speaker so she could continue stirring the stew she was warming up for lunch, and the conversation caught Charles' attention. "What difference does it make where the car is?" Charles asked. "Maybe the guy is family and he borrowed her car, or maybe he went shopping for her."

"I don't know," Sophie responded, hearing Charles' comment. "He didn't look like any family I'd want to have."

"My unsolicited advice," Charles began, "would be for you women to pull in your antennae and get out of this newcomer's business."

"My feeling exactly," a male voice on Sophie's end announced emphatically. Apparently, Sophie was using the speaker as well.

"Hi, Norman," Charles called. "Thanks for the support."

"You bet," Norman responded. "Do you two want to go into Hamilton with us tonight? A client gave me four tickets to the stage play *Moon Over the Mountain*."

Charles and Sarah looked at one another and shrugged. "Might as well," Sarah mouthed to her husband.

"We're in," Charles responded.

"We'll pick you up at 7:00," Norman replied.

Sophie had met Norman Hill the previous summer when he was making a presentation at the Cunningham Village community center. Norman was a semi-retired event planner. He owned Top of the Hill, a very successful event-planning company specializing in weddings and had attempted to retire more than once, but was always drawn back in by his love of the business.

"That will be fun," Sarah commented as she hung up. Turning to Charles, she asked, "What are your plans for the afternoon?"

"I'm going to the gym for a while and then a steam," he responded looking pleased with himself as he added, "Just as the doctor ordered."

"I think I'll come along," Sarah replied. She didn't want to work out at the gym other than spending some time on the treadmill, but the idea of lounging in the Jacuzzi after a rigorous swim in the indoor pool appealed to her.

At precisely 7:00, a Mercedes pulled up in front of the Parker's house, and Norman hopped out to open the doors for Sarah and Charles.

"Bernice's car is still missing," Sophie said once her friends were settled in the back seat.

"Charles has convinced me to mind my own business," Sarah responded with a wink.

"Okay. Come over in the morning, and we'll mind our own business together."

"It's a deal."

Norman caught Charles' eye in the rearview mirror and shook his head.

"What can you do?" Charles replied with a hopeless shrug.

A Note from the Author

I hope you enjoyed *Tattered & Torn* as much as I enjoyed writing it. This is the ninth book in A Quilting Cozy series and is followed by *Left Holding the Bag*, which includes a new friend, trunks full of vintage fabric, credit card fraud, a budding romance, and a murder—and our friends in the Cunningham Village retirement community are in the center of it all.

On page 214, I have included a preview to *Left Holding the Bag* so that you can get an idea of what our cast of characters will be involved in next.

Please let me know how you are enjoying this series. I love hearing from my readers and encourage you to contact me on my blog or send me an email.

Best wishes,

Carol Dean Jones
caroldeanjones.com
quiltingcozy@gmail.com

A Quilting Cozy Series by Carol Dean Jones

READER'S GUIDE:
A QUILTING COZY SERIES
by Carol Dean Jones

1. Delores prefers to quilt in a traditional manner because it gives her a feeling of continuity and connection to previous generations. Why do you think this was of less interest to the younger members of the club?

2. This book dealt with the search for the identity of a very old quilt. This would not have been a problem if the quilter had added a label to her quilt. What information do you think could have been on that label? If you are a quilter, do you add labels to your quilts?

3. Maud talks about the homeless shelter requirement that occupants be out on the street during the day. At eighty, she found this requirement especially difficult. What other problems do you think an elderly person might experience when living in a homeless shelter?

4. While in New Orleans, Charles was interested in touring the war museum, while Sarah preferred to go to the art museum. The problem was easily resolved, since both Sarah and Charles were accustomed to having their own personal interests in addition to those interests they shared. How do you think this helps in maintaining a healthy long-term relationship?

5. Lieutenant Stokely encourages Charles to get a PI license while Sarah continues to encourage him to get away from the stress of investigations altogether. Why is it so hard for Charles to avoid getting involved in crime solving? Do you think he should give it up entirely?